KT-545-466

3 8014 05240 6698

THE RETURN OF
MRS JONES

THE RETURN OF MRS JONES

BY

JESSICA GILMORE

MILLS & BOON

All rights reserved including the right of reproduction in whole or in part in any form. This edition is published by arrangement with Harlequin Books S.A.

This is a work of fiction. Names, characters, places, locations and incidents are purely fictional and bear no relationship to any real life individuals, living or dead, or to any actual places, business establishments, locations, events or incidents. Any resemblance is entirely coincidental.

This book is sold subject to the condition that it shall not, by way of trade or otherwise, be lent, resold, hired out or otherwise circulated without the prior consent of the publisher in any form of binding or cover other than that in which it is published and without a similar condition including this condition being imposed on the subsequent purchaser.

® and TM are trademarks owned and used by the trademark owner and/or its licensee. Trademarks marked with ® are registered with the United Kingdom Patent Office and/or the Office for Harmonisation in the Internal Market and in other countries.

First published in Great Britain 2014
by Mills & Boon, an imprint of Harlequin (UK) Limited,
Large Print edition 2014
Eton House, 18-24 Paradise Road,
Richmond, Surrey, TW9 1SR

© 2014 Jessica Gilmore

ISBN: 978-0-263-24091-7

Harlequin (UK) Limited's policy is to use papers that are natural, renewable and recyclable products and made from wood grown in sustainable forests. The logging and manufacturing processes conform to the legal environmental regulations of the country of origin.

Printed and bound in Great Britain
by CPI Antony Rowe, Chippenham, Wiltshire

For Dan.

Thanks for giving me the time to write
and always believing that I would make it.
I couldn't have done it without you. x

Special thanks must also go to my amazing
critique group, Jane, Julia and Maggie, for
three years of pep talks, brainstorming and
patience, to Merilyn for making writing fun and
to Fiona Harper and Jessica Hart for all their
encouragement and support.

CHAPTER ONE

'YOU CAN COME in, you know. Or do you city folk wear coffee patches and bypass the actual drinking process now?'

Lawrie Bennett jumped as the mocking tones jolted her out of her stunned contemplation of the ultra-modern building clinging to the harbour's edge. Turning, half convinced she had conjured up his voice along with her memories, she saw him lounging against the arty driftwood sign, the same crooked smile lurking in familiar blue eyes.

'Jonas?'

No, not a ghost. Subtle changes showed the passage of time: the surfer-blond hair was a little shorter, and a few lines round the eyes added new character to the tanned face.

Embarrassment, guilt, humiliation. Lawrie could take her pick of any of that ugly trio. Being caught hanging around outside her ex-husband's business like a gauche teenager with a crush was bad enough. To have been caught *by* her ex-husband really was a fitting end to what had been a truly terrible few weeks.

Trying to summon up an illusion of control, Lawrie switched on her best social smile—the one that had seen her through numerous meetings and charity balls. But her eyes hadn't got the 'cool and collected' memo, and flicked quickly up and down the lean body facing her.

The black tailored trousers and short-sleeved charcoal shirt were a startling change from the cut-off jeans and band T-shirt uniform of her memories, but the body underneath the sharp lines was as surfer-fit as she remembered. He still looked irritatingly good. And even worse— judging by the smirk that flared briefly in the cool eyes—he was fully aware of both her perusal and approval.

So much for control.

Jonas quirked an eyebrow. 'So, are you…planning to come in?'

How, after all this time, could his voice be so familiar? It was such a long time since she had heard those deep, measured tones tempered with a slight Cornish burr. Yet they sounded like home.

'I was just wondering if I was in the right place,' she said, gesturing at the wood and glass building behind him; so shiny and new, so unfamiliar. 'Everything's different.'

And *that,* Lawrie thought, was the understatement of the century.

'I've made some changes. What do you think?' There was pride in his voice underneath the laid-back drawl.

'Impressive,' she said. And it was. But she missed the peeling, ramshackle old building. The picturesque setting for her first job, her first kiss. Her first love. 'Did you demolish the boathouse?'

Her heart speeded up as she waited for his answer. It mattered, she realised with a shock. She hadn't set foot in the small Cornish village for nine years. Hadn't seen this man for nine years. But it still mattered.

It was her history.

'I had it relocated. It was the start of everything, after all. Demolishing the old girl would have been pretty poor thanks. And we kept the name and brand, of course.'

'Everything?' Was he talking about her? *Get a grip,* she told herself. Walking down the hill and along the harbour might have sent her spinning back in time, brought all those carefully buried memories abruptly to the surface, but by the look of the building in front of her Jonas had moved on long ago.

'So, are you coming in or not?' He ignored her question, pushing himself off the sign with the languid grace only hours balancing on a board in the rough Cornish sea could achieve. 'The coffee's excellent and the cake is even better. On the house for an ex member of staff, of course.'

Lawrie opened her mouth to refuse, to point out that the building wasn't the only thing to have changed—that, actually, she hadn't touched caffeine or refined sugar in years—but she caught a quizzical gleam in his eye and changed her mind. She wouldn't give him the satisfaction.

Besides, clean living hadn't got her very far, had it? This enforced time out was about new experiences, trying new things. There were worse places to start than a good cup of coffee brewed the way only Jonas could.

'Thank you,' she said instead.

'This way, then.' And Jonas moved to the double glass doors, holding one open for her with exaggerated gallantry. 'And, Lawrie,' he murmured as she walked past him, 'Happy Birthday.'

Lawrie froze. Just half an hour ago she had reached the sad conclusion that you couldn't get more pathetic than spending your thirtieth birthday on your own—not unless you were unemployed, single *and* alone on your thirtieth.

Lawrie was all three.

Adding an encounter with her ex really was the cherry on top of the icing on her non-existent birthday cake. She should have listened to her instincts and stayed indoors and sulked. Damn her conscience for pushing her out to get fresh air and exercise. Both were clearly overrated.

'This is where you say thank you.'

He had moved away from the door and was leading her towards a small table tucked away at the back, clearly at his ease.

'Sorry?' What was he talking about? Maybe she was in some surrealist dream, where conversation made no sense. Any second now she'd be viewing the world in black and white, possibly through the medium of mime.

'I know you've been in the city for a while...' there was an unexpected teasing note in his

voice '…but back in the real world when someone wishes you a Happy Birthday it's usual to
acknowledge them—often with a thank you.'

For the first time in over a week Lawrie felt the
heaviness lift slightly, a lessening of the burden.
'Thank you,' she said with careful emphasis. 'Of
course I *might* be trying to forget this particular
birthday.'

'Oh, yes, the big three oh.' He laughed as she
grimaced. 'It's really no big deal, once you get
used to the back ache and the knee twinges.'

'I hoped it might be like the tree falling in the
woods—if no one knows it's happening then is
it real?'

'*I* know,' he reminded her.

'Thereby foiling my cunning plan.'

A smile curved the corner of his mouth but it
didn't reach his eyes. They radiated concern. For
her. She didn't need the stab of her conscience to
tell her she didn't deserve his concern.

'Well, now it's out in the open you have to celebrate. How about a slice of my signature carrot
cake with chocolate icing? Unless, now you're a
Londoner, you prefer elaborate cupcakes? Pretty
frosting but no real substance?'

Lawrie looked up sharply. Was that some kind of cake metaphor?

'Or would you rather wait till your fiancé joins you?'

And just like that the heaviness engulfed her again. Lawrie searched for the right words, the right tone. 'Hugo and I parted ways. It seemed time for a new beginning.'

'Again?'

There was a lifetime of history in that one word. More than Lawrie could cope with this day, this week. At all.

Coming back had been a mistake. But she had nowhere else to go.

Lawrie hadn't exactly spent the last nine years planning how she'd react if she bumped into her ex-husband, but if she *had* spent time imagining every possible scenario she doubted—short of falling at his feet—that she could have come up with a situation as humiliating as this.

She looked around, desperately searching for a change of subject. 'The café looks amazing.'

It really did. She was standing in an open-plan space, with the driftwood counter along its far end and the blue walls a reminder of the ever-present sea. The real thing was a stunning back-drop framed through dramatic floor-length windows. It was all very stylish—beautiful, even—but once again Lawrie felt a pang of nostalgia for the small, homespun bar she had known.

The season was not yet fully started, but the café was buzzing with mothers and small children, groups of friends and the ubiquitous surfers. There were no menus. The day's choices were chalked up on boards displayed around the spacious room and notices proclaimed the café's values—local, organic and sustainably sourced food.

A flare of pride hit her: *he's done it—he's realised his dreams.* Long before celebrity chefs had made local food trendy Jonas had been evangelical about quality ingredients, sourcing from local farms, and using only free-range eggs in his legendary fry-ups.

'I'm glad you approve. So, what will it be?'

For one second Lawrie wanted to startle him, order something he wouldn't expect. Prove that actually she *had* changed in nine years—changed a lot. But the temptation to sink into the comfort of the past was too much. 'Skinny latte with cinnamon, please. And if you have the carrot cake in…?' She peered up at the menu board, running her eyes over the long list of tasty-looking treats.

'Of course I have it in.'

Jonas turned away to deliver her order, but Lawrie could have sworn she heard him say, 'It *is* your birthday after all.'

She was still there. Jonas tried to keep his concentration on the screen in front of him but all his attention was on the cake-eating occupant at the small table below.

The mezzanine floor that housed his office was situated directly over the kitchens, shielded from the café with blue-tinted glass that gave him privacy whilst allowing him to look out. Some days he was so busy that he completely forgot where he was, and he would look up and notice the chattering people tucking in below in complete surprise. There were bigger offices at his hotel but he preferred it here. Where it had all begun.

'Jonas? Are you listening to me?'

He jumped. 'Of course,' he lied.

'You didn't even hear me come in! Honestly, Jonas, if I want to be ignored I'll stay at home and ask my husband to clean.'

'Sorry, Fliss, I was engrossed in this email.'

Fliss peered over his shoulder. 'I can see why. It's not every day you get offered a million pounds just for letting somebody borrow your bank account, is it?'

Damn spam. 'The spam filter should be picking these up. I was just wondering why it's not working.'

She shot him a sceptical look. 'Delete that and turn your formidable mind to a real problem for a change. Suzy has been ordered to keep her feet up for the rest of her pregnancy and won't be able to project-manage Wave Fest for us.'

'Pregnancy?' He looked up in shock. 'I didn't know Suzy was expecting.'

'I expect she was keeping it a secret from you, knowing your less than enlightened views on working mothers,' Fliss said drily.

Jonas raised an eyebrow for one long moment, watching her colour with some satisfaction. 'I have no view on working mothers—or on working fathers, for that matter, I just expect my employees to pull their weight at *work*—not be at home with their feet up. Damn! There's only a month to go and we'll never get anyone to take over at this short notice. Fliss, is there any way you can take this on?'

'I don't think so.' The petite redhead was contrite. 'I still have a lot to do with the last café you bought, and if you do take over The Laurels I'll need to start on the rebrand there too. I can help with the PR—I usually do most of that anyway—but I cannot project-manage an entire festival. Suzy has all the information written out and timetabled, so at least all we need is someone to step in and run it.'

Jonas acknowledged the truth of Fliss's statement. Her workload was pretty full-on right now. He pushed his chair back and swivelled round, staring down sightlessly on the room below. 'Think, Fliss—is there anyone, any summer jobber, who's capable of taking this on?'

She stood lost in thought, concentration on her face, then shook her head. 'Nobody springs to mind.'

Jonas grimaced. 'We'll just have to bite the

bullet and get a temp in—though that's far from ideal.'

It had been hard enough handing the festival over to Suzy when it and the rest of the business had got too big for him to manage comfortably alone, even with Fliss's support. Letting a stranger loose on such an important event was impossible to imagine.

But he couldn't see another way.

Fliss was obviously thinking along the same lines. 'A temp? That will take at least a week, *and* cost a fortune in agency fees.'

'Bringing outsiders in is never easy, but it looks like we have no choice. You and I will have to keep it all ticking over until we find somebody. We managed the first three, after all…'

She flashed a conspiratorial grin at him. 'Goodness knows how. But we were young and optimistic then—and they were a lot smaller affairs; we are victims of our own success. But, okay, I'll let Dave know I'm working late so he'd better come here for dinner. Again. We were going to come back for Open Mic Night anyway.'

'Great. You drive straight over to Suzy's and go over all those lists and spreadsheets with her.

We'll divvy up tasks later. Have another think about anyone internally, and if there really is nobody I'll call a couple of agencies later today.'

A sense of satisfaction ran through him as he made the decision. He was a hands-on boss—too hands-on, some said—but he liked to know exactly how everything was handled, from salad prep to food sourcing. It was his name over the door after all.

Fliss saluted. 'Yes, Boss,' she said, then turned round to leave the room, only to stop with a strangled cry. 'Jonas! Look—in that corner over there.'

'Why exactly are you whispering?' Although he knew exactly what—exactly *who*—she had seen. He cocked an eyebrow at her, aiming for a nonchalance he didn't feel. Lawrie's unexpected presence was no big deal. He had no intention of letting it become one.

Fliss obviously had other ideas. Her eyes were alight with excitement. 'It's Lawrie. *Look*, Jonas.'

'I know it's Lawrie, but I still don't know why you're whispering. She can't hear you, you know.'

'Of course she can't, but…' Her voice turned accusatory. 'You knew she was here and didn't tell me?'

'It slipped my mind—and it's obviously slipped yours that we were discussing a rather pressing work matter.' His tone was cool. 'Don't you have somewhere to be?'

'Five minutes?' Fliss gave him a pleading look. 'I can't *not* say hello.'

To Jonas's certain knowledge Fliss hadn't seen or spoken to Lawrie in nine years. What difference would a few hours make? But his second-in-command, oldest employee and, despite his best efforts to keep her out, best friend was looking so hopeful he couldn't disappoint her.

He wasn't the only person Lawrie had walked out on.

'Five minutes,' he allowed, adding warningly, 'But, Fliss, we have a lot to do.'

'I know. I'll be quick—thank you.' Fliss rushed from the room, casting him a grateful glance over her shoulder as she did so. Less than a minute later she had arrived at Lawrie's table, falling on her in a breathless heap.

Jonas watched as Fliss sat down at the table. He saw Lawrie look up in slight confusion, her puzzled expression quickly change to one of happiness, and the mobile features light up with enthusiasm as she greeted her friend.

When they both looked up at the office he looked away, despite knowing that they couldn't see through the tinted glass; he had far too much to do to watch them catch up.

Jonas pulled up a report he had commissioned on the small chain of restaurants in Somerset he was considering taking over and read it.

After ten minutes he was still on the first page.

He glanced over at the window. They were still yakking away. What on earth had they got to talk about for so long?

Typical Lawrie. Turning everything upside down without even trying.

When he had seen her standing outside, looking so uncharacteristically unsure, he had seized the opportunity. As soon as he'd known she was back—heard through the village grapevine that she was here to stay, that she was alone—their moment of meeting had been inevitable. Trengarth was too small for a run-in not to be a certainty, but when it came he'd wanted it to be on his terms.

After all, their parting had been on hers.

Inviting her in had felt like the right thing to do. The mature thing. Maybe he should have left her outside after all.

He looked back at the computer screen and started again on the first line. It was gobbledy-gook.

Jonas's jaw set in determination. If Fliss had forgotten that she had a lot to do, he hadn't—and he was going to go down there and tell her. Right now.

At first Lawrie hadn't recognised the small red-head hurtling towards her. Nine years ago Fliss had sported a pink bob and multiple piercings and wouldn't have been seen dead in the smart black trousers and blouse she was wearing today, but the generous smile and the mischievous twinkle in the hazel eyes were just the same. After five minutes' excited chatter it was as if they were still teenage waitresses, hanging out after work, although so many things had changed Lawrie could barely keep up.

'You've been working for Jonas all this time?' Try as she might, she couldn't keep the incredulous tone out of her voice. 'What about acting and RADA?'

'Turns out I am a great amateur.'

Lawrie looked sharply at her but Fliss was still smiling, and there was no hint of disappointment in the candid eyes. 'I am also a great brand and marketing manager—who would have thought it?'

'But you wanted to do so much—had so many plans.'

'I *have* so much! Wait till you meet Dave. He moved here after you left, came for a week's surfing and never left.'

The two girls giggled conspiratorially.

'I have my drama group, and I love my job. I may not have done the travelling or the big city thing, but I have everything I need and want. I'm a lucky girl. But *your* plans sound exciting. New York! I have always wanted to live there—starring on Broadway, of course.'

So she might have made New York sound like a done deal rather than a possibility, but Lawrie had had to salvage pride from somewhere.

She was considering her reply when a shadow fell across the table. Glancing up, she saw a stern-looking Jonas standing there, a frown marring the handsome face. An unexpected flutter pulled at Lawrie's stomach, one she'd thought long dead, and she took a hurried gulp of her coffee, avoiding both his eye and Fliss's sudden speculative gleam.

'I thought you were off to see Suzy?' His attention was all on Fliss.

'I am,' Fliss protested. 'But I have just had a brainwave. How about Lawrie?'

Lawrie's grip tightened on her cup. She could feel her cheeks heating up.

'How about Lawrie, what?' Jonas asked impatiently.

It was odd, being back with the two of them and yet apart, now an outsider. Lawrie took a deep breath and leant back in her chair, affecting a confidence she was far from feeling.

'For Wave Fest, of course. No—listen,' Fliss said, jumping to her feet and grabbing Jonas's arm as he turned dismissively away. 'She's on gardening leave for the rest of the summer.'

'Gardening *what*?' He stopped and looked back at the table, catching Lawrie's eye, a sudden glint of a humour in the stern blue eyes.

She knew exactly what he was thinking—knew that he was remembering her ability to kill every plant with a mixture of forgetful indifference and remorseful over-watering.

'Is this some sort of corporate environmental thing? Time to learn how to garden?'

'No, it's a set period time to serve out your notice away from the office,' Lawrie said, her own eyes warming in response to his and her pulse speeding up as his amused gaze continued to bore into her. 'I'm on paid leave until the end of September.'

'And she's planning to stay in Cornwall most of that time,' Fliss interjected.

'Well, yes. I am. But I'm arranging my next move. I'll be travelling back and forth to London a lot—possibly overseas. What's Wave Fest, anyway?'

'Oh, Lawrie, you remember the festival Jonas and I started, don't you?'

'Actually, Fliss, Lawrie was never at Wave Fest. She was on work placements for the first two.'

The humour had left Jonas's face. It was as if the sun had unexpectedly disappeared behind a cloud. He didn't say the words she knew he was thinking. She had left before the third.

'I know we're desperate, but Lawrie's a solicitor, not a project manager—and she knows nothing about festivals.'

'But we need someone organised who can get things done and she can do that all right. Plus, she's here and she's available.'

'Fliss, you said yourself that at this time of year organising Wave Fest is a full-time job. If Lawrie's got to sort out a move—' the sharp blue eyes regarded Lawrie for an intent moment before flicking away '—she won't be able to dedicate the time we need to it.'

'Yes, for *me* it would be full time, because I have a neglected husband and the work of three people to do anyway, but Lawrie's used to city hours—this will be a relaxing break for her!'

It was almost amusing, listening to them bicker over her as if she wasn't there. Lawrie took another sip of her coffee, letting the words wash over her. After the shock of the last week it felt nice to be wanted, even if it was for a small-time job she had no intention of doing.

Suddenly she was aware of an extended silence

and looked up to find two pairs of eyes fixed on her expectantly.

'What?'

'I was just asking why you are on leave?' Jonas said, with the exaggerated patience of somebody who had asked a question several times already. 'If "gardening leave" means you're serving out your notice then you must be leaving your firm—why?'

The all too familiar sense of panic rose up inside her, filling her chest with an aching, squeezing tension. None of this was real. It was some kind of terrible dream and she would soon wake up and find Hugo snoring beside her and her pressed suit hung on the wardrobe door opposite, ready for another day at work, doing a job she was darned good at.

'I felt like a change,' she said, choosing her words carefully. 'They were offering good severance deals and I thought, what with turning thirty and everything, that this could be a good opportunity for a new start. After all, it seems silly to specialise in international law and never spend time abroad. I have lots of contacts in New York, so that seems like the logical choice.'

She had repeated the words so often to herself that she almost believed them now.

'That sounds amazing,' breathed Fliss, but Jonas looked more sceptical.

'You deviated from that all-important ten-point plan? Wasn't thirty the year you should have made partner?'

He remembered the plan. Of *course* he remembered it—she had gone over it with him enough, been teased about it enough. *'Lawrie needs to make a plan before we go out for a walk,'* he used to tell people.

She took a deep breath and forced a casual tone into her voice. 'People change, Jonas. I followed the plan for long enough, and it was very successful, but I decided that now I'm single again it might be time to see something of the world and enhance my career at the same time. It's no big deal.'

He raised an eyebrow but didn't pursue the point.

'But you won't be able to start your new job until after September so you *are* free to help out with Wave Fest.' Fliss wasn't giving up.

'Fliss, Lawrie isn't interested in the festival;

she has a job to find. Plus, if she's still being paid by her firm then she won't be able to work for us—will you?'

'I'm not sure,' she said. 'It's not law, so it's not a conflict of interest, but I don't think I can take paid work whilst on gardening leave. I'll have to check the contract, but it would be unusual if it was allowed.'

'Volunteer! We could pay your expenses and it would look great on your CV, using your time to help out with a charity event. Come on, Lawrie. It's total serendipity, you being here just when we need you. You can't argue with fate!'

'Fliss!'

Jonas was sounding annoyed, but the word 'volunteer' had struck a chord with Lawrie. She tuned the pair out.

She liked to keep busy, and the thought of spending the forseeable future with nothing to do but job-hunt terrified her. Besides, her CV was already with the best recruiters in the business, so there was little she could do until they got in touch. Most importantly she had been racking her brains, searching for a likely explanation for her sudden departure from Forrest, Gable & Garner that prospective employers would find accept-able—laudable, even. If she could tell them that she'd taken the opportunity of severance to help out with a charity festival surely that would stand her in good stead? Every company liked a bit of free CSR in these straitened times.

Okay, it wasn't part of the ten-point plan, but which part of the last few weeks *had* been? Not finding Hugo labouring over his naked secretary, not watching the senior partners close ranks as they took his side and forced her out with a nice settlement and a good reference for keeping her mouth shut.

She had returned to Trengarth to lick her wounds, to regroup. Why not wring something positive out of her situation?

'Please?' Fliss looked pleading. 'Come on, Lawrie, you'll be perfect.'

'I'll do it.' The words left her mouth before she knew exactly what she was going to say.

Fliss squealed and flung her arms around Law-rie, but Jonas took a step back, his mouth tight, his eyes unreadable.

What have I done?

'If that's okay with you, of course, Jonas,' she

added, not entirely sure what she wanted his answer to be—whether he would give her a get-out clause she didn't even know she needed. But he didn't answer—just continued to look at her with the same cool, steady regard.

Fliss jumped in before the silence stretched too far, got too awkward. 'It's fine, isn't it, Jonas? This is *fantastic*! I was going to get all the stuff from Suzy today, but why don't you come with me and meet her? Is tomorrow okay? Oh, Lawrie, it'll be just like old times, us working together.'

Fliss beamed at Lawrie, who couldn't help but smile back. Her old friend's joy was infectious.

'It looks like that's settled, then.' Jonas's face was still blank, his voice cool and professional. 'Lawrie, I'll chat to you tomorrow and go over the work involved, discuss how this will work as a volunteering role. Be sure this is something you can take on, though. Wave Fest raises tens of thousands for local charities. If you can't manage it it's imperative you let us know sooner rather than later.'

He sounded dismissive—as if he was expecting her to fail, to walk away.

How dared he? She'd negotiated million-pound contracts, painstakingly going over every single word, scrutinising each clause, routinely working sixty-hour weeks, often on short notice. One month sorting out a small local event would hardly tax her.

She lifted her head and looked straight at him, matching him cool glance for cool glance, every bit the professional, well-trained lawyer. 'I'm sure I'll manage. I like to see things through.'

He kept her gaze, scorn filling the blue eyes, turning them ice-cold. 'I'm sure you've grown up,' he said. 'But if there's a chance you'll get a job and leave before the contract ends I need to know. Promises aren't enough.'

She swallowed down her rage. If she had learnt anything from long hours of negotiating complex contracts it was how to keep her temper, no matter what the provocation. If he wanted to judge her on events that had happened nine years ago, so be it.

But she *had* promised to love him till death did them part. And that promise she had broken.

Did she actually need this hassle? The sensible thing would be to walk away, right now, lock up the cottage and go back to London. But then what? She had nowhere to live, nothing to do. At least in Cornwall she had a house, and now a way to occupy her time whilst finding the perfect job, getting her life back to the calm, ordered way it was supposed to be. And if that meant showing Jonas Jones that he was wrong—that the past wasn't as clear-cut as he obviously thought— well, that was just a bonus.

She smiled sweetly into the freezing eyes.

'I'll need to take time to sort out my move, of course,' she said, proud that her voice was steady. 'And there is a chance that I may need to travel abroad for interviews. But there will be plenty of notice. There shouldn't—there *won't* be a problem.'

'Then I'll see you tomorrow.'

The interview was clearly over.

'Enjoy the rest of your birthday.'

Fliss looked up in shock. 'It's your *birthday*? Here I am, thinking about spreadsheets and emails and offices, and what I should be doing is ordering you a cocktail to go with that cake. What are you doing later? I'm sure you have plans, but we could meet here for cocktails first?'

Lawrie's first instinct was to lie—to claim company, plans, unavailability. But Jonas had stopped, turned, was listening, and she couldn't let him know she was ashamed of her lone state. 'Actually, Fliss, I was planning a quiet one this year. I have a nice bottle of red and a good book saved up.'

It was the truth, and she had been looking forward to indulging in both. So why did it feel like a confession?

'A good book? I know you've been gone a long time, but nobody changes *that* much. Of *course* we're going to celebrate. I'll see you here for cocktails at seven, and then there's Open Mic Night later. Perfect! Jonas, you can pick her up. We don't want the birthday girl to be late.'

'Honestly—' Lawrie began, not sure what panicked her more: Jonas picking her up like old times, the chance that she might let her guard down after a cocktail, or spending her thirtieth birthday with the same people who had celebrated her eighteenth. 'I'll be fine.'

'Don't be silly.' Jonas's expression was indecipherable, his voice emotionless. 'Fliss is right. You can't spend your birthday alone. Besides, you used to enjoy singing. It'll be just like old times.'

And that, thought Lawrie, was exactly what she was afraid of.

CHAPTER TWO

'SO THIS IS where you're hiding.'

Jonas looked far too at home as he rounded the corner of Gran's cottage. And far too attractive in a pair of worn jeans that hugged his legs in all the right places, and a plain grey T-shirt emphasising his lean strength. 'I thought you had run away.'

'I thought about it,' Lawrie admitted, tugging at the hem of her skirt self-consciously.

It shouldn't take a grown woman two hours to get ready for a few drinks and some badly played guitar, and yet Lawrie had found herself paralysed by indecision. Her clothes were too conservative, too expensive, more suited to a discreet yet expensive restaurant or a professional conference than a small Cornish village.

In the end she had decided on a dress that was several years old—and several inches shorter than she usually wore.

Taking a deep breath, she pulled her hands away from the skirt and tried to remember the speech she had painstakingly prepared earlier, rehearsed at length in the shower.

'Thanks for coming to collect me—it's very nice of you. I know Fliss kind of forced your hand—' Lawrie stopped, her cheeks warm, the speech gone. 'Actually, she forced your hand in several ways earlier, and I should have thought... If you don't want me around—if it's awkward, I mean—then I'll tell her I can't do it.' She stumbled to a stop.

Great—in her former life fluency had been one of her trademarks. It looked as if she had lost that along with everything else.

'Fliss thinks she gets her own way, but if I didn't want you working for us you wouldn't be.' The blue eyes held hers for a moment. 'She's right. You'll do a good job—and, let's face it, we are a bit desperate. Beggars can't be choosers.'

Charming. It wasn't the most ringing endorsement she'd ever heard.

'I just don't want our past relationship to be an issue.' Lawrie was aware of how pompous she sounded. She'd been trying for offhand. A smirk at the corner of his mouth confirmed she had failed.

'We're both mature adults,' Jonas pointed out. 'At least I am. And it's your significant birthday we're celebrating, so hopefully you are too. I'm sure we can work together without too much bloodshed. In fact...' He moved away from the cottage and sauntered gracefully over the lawn towards her, a flat tissue-wrapped square in his hand. 'Happy Birthday.'

Lawrie stared at the proffered parcel in shock.

'Take it. It won't bite,' he teased. 'I promise. Think of it as a peace offering and a birthday present in one.'

He moved closer until he was standing next to her, leaning against the balcony, looking down on the curve of beach and sea below.

After a moment's hesitation Lawrie took the present, taking a moment to enjoy the thrill of the unknown. It was her only present, after all.

'Your gran always had the best view in the village,' Jonas said. 'It's so peaceful up here.' He shot her a glance. 'I meant to write after she died, send a card... But I didn't really know what to say. I'm sorry.'

She turned the parcel round in her hands. 'That's okay. I think people were upset we had the funeral so far away, but she wanted to be buried next to Grandpa...' Her voice trailed away and there was a sudden lump in her throat. It had been six months since the funeral but the pain of loss still cut deep. 'I wish I had telephoned more, visited more.'

'She was very proud of you.'

Lawrie nodded, not trusting herself to speak. Swallowing back the tears, she turned her attention to the present, wanting to change the subject.

She slid her finger along the fold in the tissue, pulling the tape off slowly as she went, carefully opening the paper out to reveal a silk scarf the colour of the sea below. 'It's beautiful!'

His voice was offhand. 'It always used to be your favourite colour.'

'It still is.' She looked over at him, ridiculously overcome despite his casualness. *He'd remembered.* 'You really didn't need to, but thank you, Jonas.'

'No problem.' The blue eyes swept over her assessingly. 'It matches your dress.'

'I'll go and put it on. I won't be long.'

Walking through the back door, Lawrie felt yet again as if she had gone back in time—as if she was once again her sixteen-year-old self, skipping in to say goodbye to Gran before heading out on a date, full of possibilities, full of life and desperately, achingly in love.

Only there was no Gran.

And the world no longer felt full of possibilities. She was all too aware of her limits.

Oh, to be sixteen again, walking on the beach at night after her shift ended, unable to believe that her handsome boss had asked her if she fancied a stroll. She still remembered the electric shock that had run through her when his hand had first bumped against hers. The tightness in her stomach when his long, cool caressing fingers had encased hers. The almost unbearable anticipation drying out her throat, weakening her knees, setting every single nerve-end ablaze as she waited for him to kiss her. And, *oh...!* The almost unbearable sweetness when he finally, oh so slowly, lowered his mouth to hers as the waves crashed against the shore.

It had been Lawrie's first kiss and for five

years she hadn't thought she would ever kiss anyone else.

I haven't thought about that in years. She pushed the memory of vivid, haunting dreams filled with waves, passion and familiar blue eyes firmly to one side.

She glanced up at the wall, where a framed photo hung. A much younger Lawrie looked out from it, her hair whipped by the wind and framing her face in a dark, tangled cloud, laughing, her eyes squinting against the sun. Jonas had taken it twelve years ago, on her eighteenth birthday—their wedding day.

It was all such a long time ago. Who would have thought then that they would end up like this? Apart, near-strangers, exchanging polite remarks and stiff smiles. If she'd known what lay ahead would she have made the same choices... the same mistakes?

Lawrie shook her head wildly, trying to clear the questions from her mind. She couldn't allow this temporary setback to derail her, to make her question her choices, her past. It was time to face her future—and if the plan had gone awry...well, she would tweak it.

But first her birthday. She needed—she *deserved* some fun. Maybe she could relax—just a little, just for a short while. Maybe Lawrie Bennett was allowed to let go for just one evening.

It was one of Jonas's favourite things, watching the Boat House being transformed from a family-friendly, light and airy café to an intimate bar. It was more than the deepening dusk outside the dramatic picture windows, more than the tea lights on the tables, more than the bottles of beer and wine replacing the skinny lattes, the tapas in place of cream teas.

It was the way the atmosphere changed. Grew heavier, darker. Full of infinite possibilities.

Tonight was the monthly Open Mic Night—a tradition carried through from the earliest days. Before he'd held a bar licence he used to invite friends over to the café after-hours to jam; he'd always fancied himself as a pretty mean guitarist. Once he'd licensed the premises it had become more of an organised event, yet still with a laid-back, spontaneous feel.

Folk violinists rattling out notes at an impossible speed, grungy rock wannabes, slow and

sweet soul singers—there were no exclusions. If
you had an instrument and you wanted to play,
you could sign up. There was a magic about Open
Mic Night, even after all these years. The room
might be full of regulars but there were usually
one or two surprises.

And yet tonight he was wound tight, the tension
straining across his shoulders and neck. Even
the familiar feel of the sharp strings under his
fingertips, the crowded tables, the appreciative
applause, the melding and blending of notes and
beats and voices couldn't relax him.

His eyes, his focus, were pulled to the small
table in the corner where Lawrie perched, toy-
ing with a glass of champagne, her head resting
on her hand, her eyes dreamy as she listened.
The dim lighting softened her; she looked like
his teen bride again, her dark hair loose, curling
against her shoulders, her huge grey eyes fixed
unseeingly on the stage.

On *him*.

A reluctant tug of desire pulled deep down. It
was definitely the memories, the nostalgia, he
told himself grimly. Why was she back? Why
had Lawrie Bennett, the girl who put her work,

her career, her plans before everything and everyone, given up her job and moved back?

And why did she look so scared and vulnerable?

It was none of his business—*she* was none of his business. She had made that clear a long time ago. Whatever trouble Lawrie was in she could handle it herself. She always had.

Resolutely he tore his gaze away, focussed on the room as a whole, plastering on a smile as the song ended and the room erupted into applause. Jonas exchanged an amused look with his fellow musicians as they took an ironic bow before vacating the stage for the next musicians—a local sixth form experimental rock band whose main influences seemed to be a jarring mixture of eighties New Romanticism and Death Metal.

Maybe he was getting old, Jonas thought as he made his way back to the bar. It just sounded like noise to him.

'I should be getting home.' Lawrie got to her feet and began automatically to gather the glasses and bottles. Just like old times. She stilled her hands, looking around to see if anybody had noticed.

'Don't be silly—the night is just beginning,' Fliss said in surprise.

Lawrie looked pointedly at the people heading for the door, at the musicians packing away their instruments, at vaguely familiar faces patting Jonas on the back with murmurs about babysitters, getting up for work and school runs. Since when had most of his friends had babysitters and office hours to contend with? The surf-mad mates of his youth had matured into fathers, husbands and workers. The night might feel like a step back in time, but everything had changed.

'This is the fun bit,' Fliss said, grabbing a tray filled with lurid-coloured drinks from the bar and handing a neon blue one to Lawrie. 'We get to hog the stage. What do you want to start with?'

Several pairs of eyes turned expectantly to Lawrie and she swallowed, her mouth dry. She took a sip of the cocktail, grimacing at the sweet yet almost medicinal taste. 'You go ahead without me. I don't really sing.'

'Of *course* you sing! You always used to.'

'That was a long time ago. Honestly, Fliss, I'd rather not.'

'But...'

'I thought all lawyers sang,' Jonas interceded.

Lawrie shot him a grateful glance. Fliss was evidently not going to let the point go.

'Didn't you have a karaoke bar under your office?'

'Sadly I didn't work with Ally McBeal.' Lawrie shook her head, but she was smiling now. 'The only singing I have done for years is in the shower. I'd really rather listen.'

'You heard her. And she *is* the birthday girl.'

'Which is why she shouldn't be sitting there alone,' Fliss argued. She turned to Lawrie pleadingly. 'Just do some backing vocals, then. Hum along. This is the fun part of the night—no more enduring schoolboy experiments or prog rock guitar solos. Thank goodness we limit each act to fifteen minutes or I reckon *he* would still be living out his Pink Floyd fantasies right now. There's only us here.'

Lawrie hesitated. It had been such a long time—part of the life she had done her best to pack away and forget about. Small intimate venues, guitars and set lists had no place in the ordered world she had chosen. Could she even hold a tune any more? Pick up the rhythm?

Once they had been a well-oiled machine—
Fliss's voice, rich, emotive and powerful, trained
for the West End career she had dreamed of, filling the room, and Lawrie's softer vocals, which
shouldn't really have registered at all. And then
there had been Jonas. Always there, keeping
time. There'd been times when she had got lost
in the music, blindly following where he led.

The thought of returning there was terrifying.
Lawrie shivered, goosebumps rippling up her
bare arms, and yet she acknowledged that it was
exciting too. On this night of memory and nostalgia, this moment out of time.

And how lost could she get if she stuck closely
to backing vocals? Stayed near Fliss, away from
Jonas and that unreadable expression on his face?
Did he wish she would just leave? Stay? Or did
he simply not care?

Not that there was any reason for him to care.
She had made sure of that.

She took another sip of her cocktail, noticing
with some astonishment that the glass was nearly
empty. She should be thinking about Hugo, Lawrie told herself. Mourning him, remembering

their relationship so very recently and brutally ended—not mooning over her teenage mistakes. If she was going to work here, survive here, she couldn't allow her past to intimidate her.

'Okay,' she said, putting the now empty glass down on the table and reaching for another of Fliss's concoctions—this time a sickly green. 'Backing vocals only. Let's do it.'

She was seated on the other side of the stage, angled towards the tables, so that all he could see was the fall of her hair, the curve of her cheek. Not that he was attracted to her—he knew her too well. Even after all this time. It was just that she seemed a little lost, a little vulnerable…

And there had been a time when Jonas Jones had been a sucker for dark-haired, big-eyed, vulnerable types.

He'd learned his lesson the hard way, but a man didn't want to take too many chances—not on a night filled with ghosts. He looked around, half expecting to see the creamy painted wooden slats of the old boathouse, the rough floorboards, the mismatched tables. But a twinge in his fingers brought him back to the present, reminding him that he was no longer nineteen and that, although thirty-two was certainly not old, he was too old to be playing all night on a work night.

His mouth twitched wryly. Once a work night had meant nothing. His hobbies and his job had blended into one perfect hedonistic existence: the bar, the music, the surf. He didn't know what had infuriated his parents more. How successful his beach shack had quickly become or how effortless he had made it look.

But in those days it *had* been effortless.

It wasn't that easy any more. Would his parents be proud or smug if they knew how many of the things he loved he had given up for success? Or would they still think it was not enough.

Maudlin thoughts. A definite sign that it was late, or that he'd allowed Fliss to make the cocktails again.

Time to wrap things up.

Only Fliss had started another song, carefully picking out the tune on her guitar. The breath caught in his throat. His heart was a painful lump blocking its passage.

Not this song. Not this night. Not on what could

have been, *should* have been, their twelfth wedding anniversary.

There was only so much nostalgia a man could take.

And then Lawrie picked up the tune and he was plunged into a whole other level of memory. Her voice wasn't the strongest—nothing in comparison to Fliss's—yet it had a true, wistful quality that tore at him, hooked him in, wringing truth out of the plaintive words.

Despite it all Jonas found himself playing the harmony, his hands surely and smoothly finding the right notes. They hadn't forgotten. He still knew—still felt every note, every beat, every word. How long was it since he had played this song? Not since Lawrie had left. Not even in the last desperate year of their marriage as he had watched her retreat further and further away, her eyes, her focus, firmly fixed on the gleaming spires of Oxford.

Suddenly simple folk tunes hadn't been her thing at all.

Yet she still knew all the words.

It was as if her whole body thrummed with the music. Her blood, her heartbeat, the pulses at her neck and her wrists. Long after the guitars had been packed away, the last few glasses cleared, the final lurid cocktail poured away—no one had felt able to risk the neon orange, not at past one in the morning—the beat still possessed her.

How had she managed to spend the last nine years without music? Had they even had music in the house? Music to listen to simply for the thrill it evoked deep down inside? There had been a stylish digital radio permanently tuned in to Radio Four, occasionally switched to Classic FM when they entertained. And Lawrie had attended concerts for corporate purposes—just as she had been to countless sporting events, black tie galas, charity auctions.

After a while they all blended together.

There was so much she had expunged from her life. Colour, impulsiveness, walking along a beach at dusk with the wind blowing salt-tinged tendrils of hair into her face. Enjoying the here and now.

She might have chosen a controlled, sleek, beige, stone and black existence. It didn't mean that she hadn't occasionally hungered after something a little more *vibrant*. But vibrancy had a price she hadn't been prepared to pay.

In the end control was worth it. It allowed you to plan, to achieve.

But, *damn*, the music had felt good. The right here, right now felt good. Even those ridiculously bright cocktails had been—well, not *good*, exactly but surprisingly palatable. Maybe coming back wasn't such a terrible thing after all.

'How are you getting back?'

Lawrie jumped, every sense suddenly on high alert. She didn't want to look Jonas in the eyes in case he read the conflicting emotions there. There had been a time when he'd been able to read her all too easily.

'I was planning to walk,' she said.

'Alone?'

'Unless there are suddenly bloodthirsty smugglers patrolling the dark streets of Trengarth I think I'll manage the mile home okay.'

'There's no lighting on your gran's road. I'd better walk you back.'

Lawrie opened her mouth to refuse—then shut it again, unsure what to say. Whether to make a joke out of it, point out that after negotiating

London streets for the past few years she thought she could manage a few twisty Cornish lanes. Whether to just say thank you.

Jonas took her silence for acquiescence and strode off towards the door. Lawrie stood indecisively, torn between a childish need to stand her ground, insist she was fine, and a sudden hankering for company—any company—on the walk back up the steep hill.

She had been all too alone these last weeks.

Without thought, almost impulsively, she followed him.

The night was warm, despite the breeze that blew in from the sea and the lack of cloud, and lit up by stars shining so brightly Lawrie could only stand and stare, her neck tilted back almost to the point of pain as she tried to take in the vast expanse of constellation-strewn night sky.

'Have you discovered a new planet?'

Lawrie ignored the sarcastic tone. 'I'm not sure I'd realise if I had,' she said. 'It's just you never see the sky like this in London. I had almost forgotten what it was like.'

Another reclaimed memory to add to the list.

Just how much had she shut out over the last nine years?

And how much could she bear to remember? To feel?

The shocking ache of memory—the whispers of 'what might have been'. If she hadn't walked in on Hugo she would still be in London, with Trengarth a million miles away from her thoughts, her ambitions, her dreams.

It was all so familiar. The dimly lit windy street, the harbour wall on one side and the shops on the other—a trendy mixture of surf-hire, arty boutiques and posh grub for the upmarket tourists who sailed or stayed in the village throughout the summer.

As they turned up the steep, hilly road that led to Lawrie's gran's house the shops became more prosaic: post office, grocer's, buckets and spades and souvenirs.

She stole a glance at the man strolling along by her side, walking up the hill with ease. He too was still the same in so many ways, and yet there was something harder, edgier. His very silence was spiky, and she had an urge to break it. To soften the mood.

'So...' Was that her voice? So tentative? She coughed nervously and tried again—this time loud, abrasive. More suited to a confrontation than casual conversation. 'Are you married? Any children?'

He didn't break stride or look at her. Just gave a quick shake of the head. 'Nope.'

'Anyone special?'

'Not at the moment.'

So there had been. *What did you expect?* she asked herself fiercely. *That he's been living like a monk for the last nine years? Would you even want that?*

She wasn't entirely sure of her answer.

'A couple of times I thought maybe that there was potential. But it was never quite enough. I'm an old-fashioned guy.' He slanted a glance at her, cold, unreadable. 'Marriage should be for ever. Failing once was bad enough...'

'We didn't fail.' But her words had no conviction. Lawrie tried again. 'We just wanted different things.'

'If that's the way you want to remember it.'

Now this *was* familiar. The flush of anger, the ache of frustration as they stood on either side of a very deep chasm. *No,* Lawrie told herself. *Don't say anything.* What was the point in dredging up old arguments, conflict that should be dead and buried?

Only she had never been able to resist the opportunity to fight her corner.

'It's the way it was.' Cool, calm. As if it didn't matter. And of course it didn't. It was history.

Only it was *her* history. Theirs.

It was her job, knowing when to argue a point, knowing when to let it lie. There was nothing to gain from rehashing the same old themes and yet she felt compelled to go on.

'There's no shame in admitting something isn't working, in moving on,' she persisted as they reached the top of the hill and turned down the hedge-lined lane that led to the cottage. The bumpy road ahead was hard to make out, lit just by the brilliant stars and the occasional light marking out driveways and gates. 'I couldn't stay here, you wouldn't move—what else could we do? It all seems to have worked out for you, though. You seem to have done well for yourself.'

'Surprised?' The mocking tone was back. 'You always did underestimate me, Lawrie.'

'I didn't! I never underestimated you!' Her whole body flushed, first with embarrassment, then with indignation. 'We grew apart, that's all. I didn't think…'

'Didn't think what?'

How could those smooth, cream-rich tones turn so icy?

'That I was too naïve, too small-town for your new Oxbridge friends?'

'Wow—way to rewrite history! You hated Oxford, hated London, disliked my friends, and refused to even consider moving away from Cornwall. It wasn't all me, Jonas. You wouldn't compromise on anything.'

He laughed softly. 'Compromise suggests some kind of give and take, Lawrie. Remind me again what *you* were willing to give up for *me*?'

'That's unfair.' She felt tired, defeated. She had just presided over the death of one relationship—did she really have to do the post mortem on this one too?

'Is it?'

The worst part was how uninterested he sounded. As if they were talking about complete strangers and not their hopeful younger selves.

'Actually, I should thank you.'

She peered at him through the star-lit darkness. 'Thank me?'

'For forcing me to grow up. To prove you, my parents, everyone who thought I was a worthless, surfing bum wrong.'

'I never thought that,' she whispered.

An image flashed through her head. A younger, softer Jonas, his wetsuit half peeled off, moulded to muscular thighs. Naked broad shoulders tapering down to a taut, perfectly defined stomach. Water glistening on golden tanned skin. Slicked-back wet hair. Board under one arm, a wicked smile on his mouth, an invitation in his eyes. A sudden yearning for the carefree boy he had been ran through her, making her shiver with longing. How had he turned into this cold, cynical man? Had she done this to him?

He laughed again, the humourless sound jarring her over-wrought nerves.

'Oh, Lawrie, does any of it matter? It was a long time ago—we were practically children. Getting married in our teens…we must have been crazy—it was always going to end in tears.'

'I suppose it was.' Her voice was tentative.

Was it? Once she'd thought they would be together for ever, that they were two halves of one
whole. Hearing him reduce their passion to the
actions of two irresponsible teenagers nearly
undid her. She fought against the lump in her
throat, fought for composure, desperate to change
the subject, lighten the mood which had turned
as dark as night.

'Here you are.'

He stopped at the gate that led into the small
driveway and Lawrie skidded to an abrupt stop—
close, but not touching him. She was achingly
aware of his proximity, and the knowledge that if
she reached out just an infinitesimal amount she
would be able to touch him made her shiver with
longing, with desire, with fear. She wanted to
look away but found herself caught in his moonlit gaze, the blue eyes silvered by the starlight.

'It wasn't all bad, though. Being a crazy teen.'

The cream had returned to his voice. His tone
was low, almost whispered, and she felt herself
swaying towards him.

'No, of course not. That was the happiest time
of my life.'

Damn, she hadn't meant to admit that—not to

him, not to herself. It must be the cocktails talking. But as the words left her mouth she realised their truth.

'The happiest time,' she whispered, so low she hoped he hadn't heard her.

Just one little step—that was all it took. One little step and she was touching him, looking up at him. Her breasts brushed against his chest and just that one small touch set her achingly aware nerves on fire. She felt the jolt of desire shock through her, buzzing through to her fingers, to her toes, pooling deep within her.

Jonas's head was tilted down. The full focus of his disconcertingly intense eyes on her. Lawrie swallowed and licked suddenly dry lips, her nails cutting into her palms as she curled them into tight fists. The urge to grab him and pull him close was suddenly almost overwhelming.

'Jonas?'

An entreaty? A question? Lawrie didn't know what she was asking him, what she was begging him for. All she knew was that it was her birthday. And that she hadn't felt this alive for a long, long time.

'Jonas…'

He stayed still for a long second, his eyes still fixed on hers, their expression unreadable.

And then he took a step back. The sudden space between them was a yawning chasm. 'Good-night, Lawrie. I'll see you in the morning. Don't be late—there's a lot to go through.'

Lawrie suppressed a shudder. It was suddenly so cold. 'I'm never late.'

'Good.'

She stood by the gate, watching as he turned and began to stride down the path, ruthlessly suppressing the part of her that wanted to call after him, run after him. Yet she couldn't ignore the odd skip her heart gave as he stopped and looked back.

'Oh, and, Lawrie… Happy Birthday.'

And then he was gone. Swallowed up by the velvety blackness like the ghost of birthdays past.

Lawrie sagged against the gatepost, an unwelcome mixture of frustrated desire and loneliness pulsing through her. If this was how one night with Jonas could make her feel, how on earth was she going to manage a whole summer?

She forced herself upright. She was vulnerable

right now, that was all. She would just have to toughen up even more—harden herself.

And stay as far away from Jonas Jones as she possibly could, boss or not.

CHAPTER THREE

LAWRIE WAS DETERMINED to be early.

'Don't be late' indeed.

Even if she *had* gone to bed long after one a.m., and even if she *had* spent half the night lying awake in a frustrated tangle of hot sheets and even hotter regrets, there was no way she was giving him the satisfaction.

Besides, she might be in Trengarth, not Hampstead, and in her old, narrow single bed and not the lumbar-adjusted super-king-size one she had shared with Hugo, but it was nice to retrieve a little of her old routine from the wreckage of the last week.

She'd been up at six sharp, showered and ready to go by seven.

So why was she still standing irresolutely in the kitchen at ten past seven, fingering the scarf Jonas had bought her? It looked good teamed with her crisp white shirt and grey pencil skirt, softening the severe corporate lines of her London work wardrobe, and yet she didn't want to give Jonas the wrong idea—come into work brandishing his colours.

She began to unknot it for the third time, then caught sight of herself in the mirror. Face drawn, anxious.

It's just a scarf, she thought impatiently, pulling the door shut and locking it behind her. *Not an engagement ring.* She looked down at her left hand, the third finger bare—bare of Hugo's exquisite princess cut diamond solitaire, of Jonas's antique amethyst twist.

Two engagement rings before turning thirty. Not bad for someone who had vowed to remain independent. Her mother had been married three times before thirty; maybe Lawrie wasn't doing so badly after all.

It was another beautiful day, with the sun already shining down from a deep blue sky completely undisturbed by any hint of cloud, and the light breeze a refreshing contrast to the deepening heat. This was Cornwall at its best—this was what she had missed on those dusty, summer days in London: the sun glancing off the sea, the vibrancy of the colours, the smell of grass, salt and beach. The smell of home.

Don't get too used to it, Lawrie told herself as she walked along the lane—a brighter, far less intimate and yet lonelier walk in the early-morning light. *This is just an interlude.* It was time to start focussing on her next step, giving those recruitment agencies a quick nudge. After all, they'd had her CV for nearly a week now. She should have plenty of free time. How much work could organising a few bands be?

Five hours later, after an incredibly long and detailed hand-over by the sofa-bound Suzy, Lawrie was severely revising her estimate of the work involved. Just when had Wave Fest turned from a few guitars and a barbecue on a beach to a three-night extravaganza?

Walking back into Jonas's office, files piled high in her arms, her head was so busy buzzing with the endless stream of information Suzy had supplied that Lawrie had almost forgotten the ending to the night before—forgotten the unexpected desire that had flared up so hotly, despite thinking about nothing else as Fliss drove her through the narrow country lanes to Suzy's village home.

But walking back into the Boat House brought the memory flooding back. She had wanted him to kiss her.

It wasn't real. This was Jonas Jones. She had been there, done that, moved on. Besides, Lawrie told herself firmly, she couldn't afford any emotional ties. She was already mentally spinning this volunteer role into a positive on her CV. This could be the way to set her aside from all the other ambitious thirty-somethings hungry for the next, more prestigious role.

Volunteering to manage a high-profile project raising money for charity—an environmental charity, at that—would add to her Oxford degree and her eight successful years at an old City firm and she would be a very promising candidate indeed. She might even have her pick of jobs.

Only, Lawrie thought as she clasped the large, heavy files more firmly, negotiating contracts was a very different skill from organising a festival. She was used to representing multiple companies who thought they had first dibs on her time *all* the time, but at least there was uniformity to the work, making it simpler to switch between clients. This was more like running an entire law firm single-handed, handling everything from divorces to company takeovers.

There didn't seem to be an aspect of Wave Fest that Suzy hadn't been in charge of—that Lawrie was now in charge of—from budgets to booking bands, from health and safety forms and risk assessment to portaloo hire.

And there was a file for each task.

Jonas was hard at work as she staggered into the office, but he swung his chair round as she dumped the heavy pile on the round conference table with a bang. His face was guarded, although she could have sworn she saw a fleeting smirk as he took in the large amount of paperwork she had lugged in.

'Changed your mind now you know what's in store?'

It was said lightly, but a muscle beating at the side of his jaw betrayed some tension. Maybe he wasn't as indifferent to her as he seemed. Or maybe it was another dig at her lack of commitment.

Stop trying to second-guess him, Lawrie. It was probably just a throwaway comment.

'No, but it's more daunting than I imagined,' she admitted honestly. 'This lot—' she gestured at the files behind her '—is just invoices, purchase orders, health and safety certificates, insurance documents. The actual work is being emailed as we speak.'

'Can you do it?'

'It's different to my usual line, and my secretary would have taken care of most of the admin-related work—but, yes, I can do it. I'll need to spend a couple of days reading this lot, though.'

'Here?'

'Sorry?'

'Are you intending to work *here*?'

Lawrie looked up, confused. Where else would she work?

Her eyes caught his. Held them. And for several long seconds she was aware of nothing but the intense blue, the flicker of heat at the heart of his gaze. She caught her breath, an ache suddenly hollowing in her chest, need mingling with the excitement clenching at her stomach. She dragged her eyes reluctantly away, loss unexpectedly consuming her as she stepped back, self-consciously pulling at a folder, looking anywhere but at him, doing her best to ignore the sudden flare of desire, her total awareness of every inch of him.

His shirt matched his eyes, was open at his throat, exposing a small triangle of tanned chest; his long legs were encased in perfectly cut charcoal trousers.

She smiled at him, making it light, trying to keep her sudden nerves hidden, her voice steady. *For goodness' sake, Lawrie, you're a professional.* 'I was planning on it. I could work at home, but it will be easier to get answers to my questions if I'm on site.'

He nodded shortly. 'I agree. That's why I thought you might be better off based at the hotel.'

'The hotel?' For goodness' sake, she sounded like an echo.

'Coombe End. I appreciate it's not as convenient as here—you won't be able to walk to work—but as it's the venue for Wave Fest it makes a lot of sense for you to spend most of your time there.'

His smile was pure politeness. He might have been talking to a complete stranger.

Lawrie shook her head, trying to clear some of

the confusion. 'You hold the festival at Coombe End? Your parents *let* you?'

She knew things had changed, but if Richard and Caroline Jones were allowing rock music and campers through the gates of Coombe End then she hadn't come back to the Trengarth she remembered. She had entered a parallel universe.

'No.' His eyes caught hers again, proud and challenging. 'They don't. *I* allow it. Coombe End belongs to me. I own it now.'

She stared at him, a surge of delight running through her, shocking her with its strength. So his parents had finally shown some belief in him.

'They gave you Coombe End? Oh, Jonas that's wonderful.'

He shook his head, his face dark, forbidding. 'They gave me nothing. I bought it. And I paid handsomely for every brick and every blade of grass.'

He had *bought* Coombe End? Lawrie looked around at the immaculately styled office, at the glass separating them from the café below, at the smooth polished wooden floor, the gleaming tiles, the low, comfortable sofas and designer chairs and tables. The whole building shouted out taste, sophistication. It shouted investment and money. She knew things had grown, changed, but how much? Whatever Jonas was doing now it was certainly more than serving up coffee and cakes to friends.

A lot more.

'That's great,' she said lamely, wanting to ask a million questions but not knowing where to start.

Besides, it wasn't any of her business. It hadn't been for a long time.

'I was planning to head over there this afternoon, so I could show you around, introduce you to the rest of the office staff. It'll probably be a couple of hours before I'm ready to leave, though, is that okay?'

Lawrie shook her head, her mind still turning over the 'rest of the office staff' comment. How many people did he employ?

'No problem. I want to go through this lot and make some notes, anyway.'

'If you're hungry just pop downstairs. Carl will make you anything you want.'

And he turned back to his computer screen, instantly absorbed in the document he was reading.

She had been dismissed. It shouldn't rankle—

this was hard enough without his constant attention. But it did.

Lawrie sat down at the table and pulled the first file towards her, groaning inwardly at the thick stack of insurance documents inside. Deciphering the indecipherable, crafting the impenetrable—those were the tools of her trade and she was excellent at it—but today her eyes were skidding over each dense sentence, unable to make sense of them. She was trying to focus all her attention on the words dancing on the page in front of her but she was all too aware of Jonas's every move—the rustle as he shifted posture, the tap of his long, capable fingers on the keyboard.

Despite herself she let her eyes wander over to him, watching him work. She tried to pull her gaze away from his hands but she was paralysed, intent, as his fingers caressed the keyboard, pressing decisively on each key.

He had always been so very good with his hands.

'Did you say something?'

'No,' she lied, hoping he hadn't turned round, hadn't seen her blush.

Please, she prayed silently, she hadn't just

moaned out loud, had she? For goodness' sake she was a grown woman—not a teenager at the mercy of her hormones. At least she'd thought she was.

It was coming home. She had been away too long and this sudden return at a time of stress had released some sort of sensory memory, turning her back into the weak-kneed teenager crushing so deeply on her boss that every nerve had been finely tuned to his every word and movement. It was science, that was all.

Science, but still rather uncomfortable.

'I'm thirsty,' she announced. 'I'll just go and get some water.'

His satirical gaze uncomfortably upon her, she slid out of the door, heading for the kitchens beneath, relieved to be released from his proximity. If she didn't get a handle on her hormones soon then she was in for a very uncomfortable few weeks.

Walking down the stairs, she pulled her phone out of her pocket, automatically checking it for messages. Just the simple act of holding it created a much-needed sense of purpose, of control.

Nothing. Not from her old colleagues, not from

her friends in London, not from Hugo. It was as if they had closed the gap her absence had created so seamlessly that nobody knew she had gone. Or if they did they simply didn't care. Yesterday had been her thirtieth birthday. She was supposed to have been having dinner with twenty of their closest friends. Other professional couples. How had Hugo explained her absence?

Or had he taken his secretary instead? His lover. After all, they had been *his* friends first.

This was the year she had been going to get around to finally organising their wedding.

This was the year they'd been going to discuss children. Not *have* them yet, obviously, but start timetabling them in.

They were supposed to have been spending the rest of their lives together, and yet Hugo had let her go without a word, without a gesture. Just as Jonas had all those years ago. Just as her mother had.

She just wasn't worth holding on to.

Lawrie leant against the wall, grateful for the chill of the tiles on her suddenly hot face. *Don't cry*, she told herself, willing away the pressure behind her eyelids. *Never cry. You don't need them—you don't need anybody.*

A large glass of iced water and some fresh air helped Lawrie recover some of her equilibrium and she returned to the office feeling a great deal better. Turning her back determinedly on Jonas, she called on all her professional resources and buried herself in the insurance folder, finding a strange calm in returning to the legalese so recently denied her. Pulling a notebook close, she began to scribble notes, looking at expiry dates, costs, and jotting down anything that needed immediate attention, losing herself in the work.

'Lawrie...? *Lawrie?*' Jonas was standing behind her, an amused glint in the blue eyes. 'Fascinating, are they?' He gestured at the folders.

'A little,' she agreed, pulling herself out of the work reluctantly. 'I'm sorry—do you need me?'

'I'm heading off to Coombe End. Do you still want me to show you around?'

Did she? What she really wanted was more time alone—more time to get lost in the work and let the real world carry on without her.

But it would be a lot easier tomorrow if she knew what to expect.

'Oh, yes, thanks.' She pushed her chair back and began to pile the folders and her closely covered sheets of paper together. 'I'll just…' She gestured at the files spread all over the table and began to pull them together, bracing herself ready to scoop them up.

'Here—let me.'

Jonas leant over and picked up the large pile, his arm brushing hers and sending a tingle from her wrist shooting through her body straight down to her toes. She leapt back.

'If you're ready?'

'Absolutely, I'll just get my bag—give me two minutes.'

'I'll meet you at the car; it's just out front.'

'Okay.'

The door closed behind him and Lawrie sank back into her seat with a sigh. She had to pull herself together. Stop acting like the gauche schoolgirl she'd outgrown years ago.

Jonas pulled his car round to the front of the restaurant, idling the engine as he waited for Lawrie.

Their first day working together was going well. He'd had a productive two hours' work just then, not thinking about and not even noticing the exposed nape of her neck, her long, bare legs, not at all aware of every rustle, every slight movement.

Well, maybe just a little aware. But they were just physical things. And Cornwall in summer was full of attractive women—beautiful women, even.

And yet during the last two hours the room he had designed, the room that had evoked light and space, had felt small, claustrophobic, airless. How could someone as slight as Lawrie take up so much space?

Jonas looked over at the Boat House impatiently, just as Lawrie emerged through the front door, a carefully blank, slightly snooty look on her face—the expression that had used to mean she was unsure of the situation. Did it still mean that? He used to be able to read her every shifting emotion, no matter how she tried to hide them.

Then one day he simply couldn't read her at all.

She stopped at the gate, peering down the road, puzzled.

What was she looking for? He half raised one

hand to wave at her, then quickly lowered it, leaning on the horn instead, with a little more emphasis than needed. He allowed himself a fleeting
moment of amusement as she jumped at the noise
and then, obviously flustered, crossed the harbour road, walking slowly towards the car.

He leant across to open the passenger door, sitting back as she slid in, looking straight ahead,
trying not to watch her legs slide down over the
seat, her round, firm bottom wriggling down
over the padded leather, the sudden definition
as the seatbelt tightened against her chest.

'Nice,' she said appreciatively, putting a hand
out to stroke the walnut dashboard as Jonas
pulled the low, sleek car away from the kerb. 'I
have to say I hadn't pegged you as a sports car
man. I was looking for the camper van.'

'Oh, this is just a runabout. I still have the
camper. There's no way I could get a board in
here.'

He laughed as she grimaced.

'You and your boards,' she said. 'If they're that
important you should have gone for a sensible
people carrier rather than this midlife crisis on
wheels.'

'Midlife crisis?' he mock-huffed. There was no way he was going to admit the secret pride he took in the car.

Jonas didn't care too much what people said, what people thought of him, but he allowed himself a little smirk of satisfaction every time he passed one of his parents' cronies and saw them clock the car and the driver and, for one grudging moment, admit to themselves that that no-good boy had done well.

'At least this has a real engine in it. I've seen that dainty little convertible you call a car. Do you actually put flowers in that holder?'

She shook her head, smiling. 'You have to admit it's convenient for parking. But I can see why you like this—she goes like a dream,' she said as he turned the corner onto the main road and the car began purring up the steep climb. 'And at least she isn't red, so not a total cliché! I'm glad that you kept the camper, though. I was always fond of the old girl. What?' she asked as he slid her a sly smile.

'I'm glad you've finally acknowledged that she's a she—you'll call her by her name next,' he teased.

'I will *never* call a twenty-year-old rusty van by such a ridiculous name—by *any* name. A car is not a person,' she said with a haughty flick of her ponytail.

But Jonas could hear the laughter in her voice as he deftly swung the car round the corner and along the narrow lanes that led to the hotel, just two coves away.

'Go on—say it,' he coaxed her.

It had been a long time since he had seen Lawrie laugh. Judging by the wounded, defensive look in her eyes it was a long time since she *had* laughed.

'I'll help. Bar… Barb…'

'No!' But she was definitely trying not to laugh, and there was a dimple at the corner of her lush, full mouth. 'What about this one? What have you named her?'

'Nice escape, Ms Bennett. But I will get you to say her name before you leave.'

'We'll see.'

The words were dismissive but she still sounded amused. Jonas sneaked a glance at his passenger and saw her face was more relaxed, her posture less rigid.

'So go on—surprise me. What's she called?'

'Ah,' he said lightly. 'This baby doesn't have a name. It'd be disloyal to the camper.'

This time she did laugh—slightly croaky, as if she were unused to making the sound, but as deep and rich, as infectious as Jonas remembered.

'We wouldn't want to hurt the feelings of a rusting old van, would we?'

'I assure her every day that I only bought this to spare her tired old axles, but I'm not sure she believes me.'

'Nobody likes being replaced by a younger model.'

There was a dark undercurrent to her tone and he glanced at her sharply, but her face was as impassive as ever, the laughter gone as if it had never been, replaced by that cool mask she always put on.

It had been her coolness that had first attracted him—the innocent look on her face as she said the most outrageous things a stark contrast to the noisy beach bums he'd been surrounded by. It had been the unexpected moments when she'd opened up that had made him fall head over heels in love with her—the moments when her mask had dropped and she'd lit up with laughter, with indignation, with passion.

Dangerous memories. His hands tightened on the wheel as he navigated the narrow bends, the hedgerows high beside them as if they were driving through a dark, tree-lined tunnel.

'I'm glad you're driving. I'm not sure I'd find my way by road,' Lawrie said conversationally, as if she were discussing the weather.

As beautifully mannered as ever, Jonas thought.

'It's been a long time since I've been to Coombe End. I can't imagine it without your parents there—how are they?'

There were a million and one responses he could give to that. Jonas settled for the most polite. 'Retired.'

Lawrie made an incredulous noise. '*Retired?* Seriously? I didn't think the word was even in their vocabulary.'

'It wasn't. It took a heart attack to make them even talk about it, and a second one to make them do it.'

'I'm sorry to hear that. What are they doing now?'

Jonas's mouth twisted wryly. Making sure he

knew just how much they regretted it. Just how much it hurt to see their profligate son undo all their hard work. Not that any of that was Lawrie's business. Not any more.

'Living in a respectable villa, in a respectable village in Dorset, and taking an inordinate amount of cruises—which they mostly complain about, of course. Still, every retiree needs a hobby.'

Lawrie looked at him, concern in the deep grey eyes. Of course she knew more about his relationship with his parents than anyone else. He wasn't used to that—to people seeing behind his flippant tone. He made damn sure that nobody did.

'I can't imagine it—your parents, of all people, taking it easy on cruise liners. How long since you bought them out?'

'Coming up to four years.' Jonas kept his answer short, terse.

'Are they still involved?'

'Now *that*, Lawrie dear, would mean them communicating with me.' All this talk of his parents—his least favourite subject. It was time to turn the tables. 'Talking about difficult relations,' Jonas said, 'how is your mother? Still in Spain?'

Lawrie twisted in her seat and stared at him. 'How did you know she was in Spain?'

Jonas grinned to himself, allowing his fingers to beat out a tune on the leather of the steering wheel. *Nice deflection, Jones.* 'I met her when she was over from Spain, introducing her new husband…John, isn't it? He seemed like a nice bloke. Didn't she come to London? She said she wanted to see you.'

Lawrie's mouth had thinned; the relaxed posture was gone. Any straighter and he could use her back as a ruler.

'I was busy.'

Jonas shrugged. 'I think this one might be different. She seemed settled, happy.'

Lawrie was radiating disapproval. 'Maybe five is her lucky number.'

'People make mistakes. Your mother certainly did. But she's so proud of you.'

'She has no right to be proud of me—she doesn't know me. And if she was so keen to see me she should have come back for Gran's funeral.'

'Didn't she?'

He should have been at the funeral too. He'd

said his own private goodbye to Gran on the day, alone at the cottage. But he should have gone.

'She was on a retreat.' It was Lawrie's turn to be terse.

Maybe it had been too successful a deflection. Jonas searched for a response but couldn't find one. Lawrie had every right to be angry, but at least her mother wanted to make amends.

His parents wouldn't have known what they were expected to make amends *for*—as far as they were concerned any problems in their relationship were all down to him.

He was their eternal disappointment.

There was an awkward silence for a few long minutes, with Jonas concentrating on the narrow road, pulling over several times as tractors lumbered past, and Lawrie staring out of the window.

'I'm sorry,' she said suddenly. 'I'm glad she's happy—that five husbands and goodness knows how many boyfriends later she's settled. But it's thirty years too late for me.'

'I know.'

And he did. He knew it all. He knew how bitter Lawrie was about her mother's desertion, how angry. He knew how vulnerable years of moving around, adapting to new homes, new schools, new stepfathers had made her.

He knew how difficult it was for her to trust, to rely on anyone. It was something he couldn't ever allow himself to forget.

When it all got too much Lawrie Bennett ran away. Like mother, like daughter. Not caring who or what she left behind.

This time he was not getting to get left in her destructive wake.

CHAPTER FOUR

'WHAT HAVE YOU done with the helipad? And didn't the ninth hole start over there? I'm not sure your father ever recovered from that lesson. Or your mother…although I *did* offer to pay for the window.'

Lawrie would have bet everything she owned that a country house hotel catering for the rich was not Jonas's style. But now she was here it was hard to pinpoint the changes she instinctively knew he must have made. Coombe End *looked* the same—a tranquil Queen Anne manor house set in stunning acres of managed woodland at the back, green meadows at the front, running into the vivid blue blur of sea on the horizon—and yet something was different. Something other than the change in owner and the apparent loss of a golf course and helipad.

Maybe it was the car park? There were a few high-end cars dotted here and there, but they were joined by plenty of others: people carriers, old bangers, small town cars and a whole fleet worth of camper vans, their bright paintwork shining brightly in the sun. Last time she had been here the car park had been filled with BMWs and Mercedes and other, less obviously identifiable makes—discreet and expensive, just like the hotel.

Lawrie hadn't seen many camper vans in London, and the sight of their cheery squat box shape, their rounded curves and white tops, filled her with a sudden inexplicable sense of happiness. Which was absurd. Camper vans were for man-boys who refused to grow up. Ridiculous, gas-guzzling, unreliable eyesores.

So why did they make her feel as if she was home?

As Jonas led Lawrie along the white gravelled path that clung to the side of the graceful old building her sense of discombobulation increased. The formal gardens were in full flower, displaying all their early summer gaudy glory—giant beds filled with gigantic hydrangea bushes, full flowered and opulent—but the gardens as a whole were a lot less manicured, the grass on the front lawns longer than she remembered, with wildflowers daring to peek out amongst the velvety green blades of grass.

And what was that? The rose garden was gone, replaced by a herb garden with small winding paths and six wooden beehives.

'You've replaced your mother's pride and joy?' she said, only half in mock horror.

'Doesn't it all look terribly untidy?' Jonas said, his voice prim and faintly scandalised, a perfect parody of his mother.

Lawrie shook her head, too busy looking around to answer him, as they walked up the sandstone steps that led to the large double doors.

The old heavy oak doors were still there, but stripped, varnished—somehow more inviting. The discreet brass plaque had gone. Instead a driftwood sign set onto the wall was engraved with 'Boat House Hotel'.

'Come on,' Jonas said, nudging her forward. 'I'll show you around.'

He stood aside and ushered her through the open door. With one last, lingering look at the sun-drenched lawn Lawrie went through into the hotel.

She hadn't spent much time here before. Jonas had left home the day he turned sixteen—by mutual agreement, he had claimed—and had slept above the bar or in the camper van before they were married. He'd converted the room over the bar into a cosy studio apartment once they were. It had always felt like a royal summons on the few occasions when they were invited over for dinner—the even fewer occasions she had persuaded Jonas to accept.

They had always been formal, faux-intimate family dinners, held on the public stage of the hotel dining room. Jonas's parents' priority had clearly been their guests, not their son and his wife. Long, torturous courses of beautifully put together rich food, hours full of polite small talk, filled with a multitude of poisoned, well targeted barbs.

Her memories made the reality even more of a shock as Lawrie walked into the bright, welcoming foyer. The changes outside had been definite, but subtle; the inside, however, was completely, obviously, defiantly different. Inside the large hallway the dark wood panelling, the brocade and velvet, had been stripped away, allowing the graceful lines of the old house to shine through in colours reflecting Jonas's love of the sea: deep blues and marine greens accentuating the cream décor.

'It's all reclaimed local materials—driftwood, recycled glass, re-covered sofas,' Jonas explained. 'And everything is Cornish-made—from the pictures on the walls to the glasses behind the bar.'

'It's amazing,' Lawrie said, looking about her at the room at once so familiar and yet so new, feeling a little like Alice falling into Wonderland. 'I love it. It's really elegant, isn't it? But not cold. It feels homely, somehow, despite its size.'

'That's the effect I wanted.' His voice was casual but his eyes blazed blue as he looked at her. 'You always did get it.'

Lawrie held his gaze for a long moment, the room fading away. That look in his eyes. That approval. Once she'd craved it, looked for it, yearned for it. Like the perfect cup of tea at the perfect temperature. A slab of chocolate exactly the right mixture of bitter and sweet. A chip, crisp and hot and salty on the outside, smooth and fluffy as you bit down.

Of course the only tea she drank nowadays

was herbal, and she hadn't had a chip—not even a hand-cut one—in years.

And she didn't need anyone's approval.

'Some of my clients own hotels,' she said, injecting as much cool professionalism into her voice as she could. 'I've seen some great examples of décor, and some fairly alarming ones too. This is really lovely, though, Jonas.'

The approval faded, a quizzical gleam taking its place, but all he said was, 'I'm glad you approve. Let's hear your professional opinion on the rest of the place. This way.'

And Jonas turned and began to walk along the polished wooden floor towards the archway that led into the main ground floor corridor.

Lawrie heaved a sigh. Of relief, she told herself sternly. Job done—professional relationship back on track.

So why did she feel as if the sun had just disappeared behind a very black cloud?

Lawrie followed Jonas through the foyer and down the corridor, watching him greet both staff and guests with a smile, a quick word, a clap on the shoulder—evident master of his empire. It was odd... He used to be so unhappy here, a stranger in his own home, and now he appeared completely at ease.

Jonas led her into the old dining room. A large, imposing space, dominated by the series of floor-to-ceiling windows along the far wall matched by a parade of pillars reaching up to the high ceiling. This room too had been extensively remodelled, with a similar look and feel to the café on the seafront, all the lace and delicate china replaced with light woods and cheerful tablecloths.

A long table ran along one end, filled with large jugs, chunky earthenware mugs and plates of small cakes and biscuits.

'Wouldn't want the guests to get hungry,' Jonas explained as he grabbed a pair of large mugs and poured coffee from one of the jugs, automatically adding milk to them before handing one to Lawrie.

She opened her mouth to decline but closed it as she breathed in the rich, dark aroma.

Why had she given up coffee? she wondered as she took a cautious sip. It was delicious, and the creamy Cornish milk was a perfect companion to the bitter nectar. Two milky coffees in two days—she was slipping back into bad habits.

The coffee was the least of it.

Jonas carried his cup over to the nearest window, which stood slightly ajar, allowing the slight summer breeze to permeate the room with the sweet promise of fresh warmth. The breeze ruffled his dark blond hair, making him look younger, more approachable.

Like the boy she had married. Was he still there, somewhere inside this ambitious, coolly confident man, that impetuous, eager boy?

Lawrie had promised herself that she wouldn't probe. The last nine years, Jonas's life, his business… None of it was relevant. Knowing the details wouldn't help her with her job. Or with the distance she needed to maintain between them. And yet curiosity was itching through her.

She wandered over to the window and stood next to him, every fibre acutely aware of his proximity. Of the casual way he was leaning against the window frame. The golden hairs on the back of his tanned wrists. The undone button at his neck and the triangle of burnished skin it revealed.

Lawrie swallowed, the hot clench at her stomach reminding her of her vulnerability, of the attraction she didn't want to acknowledge.

She looked out, following his line of sight as he gazed into the distance. The sea was clearly visible in the distance, calm and unruffled, the smell of it clear on the breeze. And the urge to know more, to know him again, suddenly overwhelmed her.

'Why here?' There—it was said.

Jonas looked mildly surprised. 'Where else? This room works well as a dining room, has good access to the kitchens. It would have been silly to change it just for change's sake.'

Lawrie shook her head. 'I didn't mean the room. I meant the whole thing,' she said, aware she was probing deeper than she had any right to. 'I mean here. You hated this place. I couldn't get you to set foot inside the gates without a massive fight. I could understand it if your parents had gifted the place to you, but if you paid full value for and then remodelled it? It must have cost a *fortune*!'

Jonas quirked an eyebrow at her. 'Oh, I get it. You're wondering about how much I'm worth. Regretting the divorce after all?'

Heat flooded through her. She could feel her cheeks reddening. 'That's not what I meant,' she protested. 'You know I wouldn't have taken a penny.'

'That's my Lawrie—still so serious.'

Jonas let out a laugh and Lawrie swatted him indignantly, trying to repress the secret thrill that crept over her at the possessive word 'my'.

'Oh, ha-ha. Very funny.'

Jonas leant back against the window pane, still grinning, and took a sip from the chunky Cornishware mug. 'You always were so easy to wind up. Good to know some things don't change.'

'So?' she pressed him, taking advantage of his suddenly companionable mood. 'How come you ended up at Coombe End?'

Jonas didn't reply for a long moment, and the mischievous glint in his eyes faded to annoyance. When he spoke his tone was clipped. 'This was my home once, Lawrie. It wasn't a big conspiracy or takeover, no matter what the village gossips say.'

Lawrie winced. She hadn't considered the inevitable fall-out the change of ownership must have caused. The whole of Trengarth—the whole area—knew how things stood between Jonas and his parents. And there were few without definite opinions on the matter.

'Since when did you care about what the gossips say?' They had always been different in that regard. She so self-conscious, he proudly indifferent.

His eyes were cold. 'I don't. My decision to buy Coombe End was purely a business one. I always knew this place could be more. Yes, it was successful—very successful—if that kind of thing appealed: a little piece of the capital by the sea. You could drive straight here, fly your helicopter here, use the private beach, play the golf course and return home without ever experiencing what Cornwall is about,' he said, his lip curling as he remembered. 'The kind of place your fiancé probably took you.'

'Ex-fiancé,' Lawrie corrected him. She shook her head, refusing to take the bait, but there was an uncomfortable element of truth to his words. Hugo had liked the luxury hotel experience, it was true, but they'd been so busy that just snatching a night away had been enough. There had never been time to explore local culture as well.

'Of course,' Jonas said, putting his mug down decisively and stepping away from the window. 'Ex. Come on. There's a lot to go through.'

No wonder she felt like Alice, being constantly hustled from place to place. She half expected Jonas to pull out a pocket watch. If there were croquet lawns she was in serious trouble.

Lawrie took a last reluctant gulp of the creamy coffee and placed her mug onto the nearest table before following Jonas once again. He led her back down the corridor, through the foyer and outside, along the winding path that led to the woods that made up most of the outside property.

One of Coombe End's winter money-makers had been shooting parties. Lawrie had hated hearing the bangs from the woods and seeing the braces of poor, foolish pheasants being carried back to the house, heads lolling pathetically.

Jonas was walking fast, with intent, and she had to lengthen her stride to keep up with him. It took her by surprise when he came to a sudden halt at the end of the gravelled path, where a long grassy track snaked away ahead of them up the small wooded hill that bordered the hotel gardens.

Lawrie skittered to an undignified stop, clamping down on the urge to grab onto him for support. 'A bit of warning would be nice,' she muttered as she righted herself cautiously.

Jonas ignored her. 'I never hated this place, Law,' he said after a while, gesturing out towards the woodland, its trees a multitude of green against the blue sky.

A secret thrill shuddered through her at the sound of the old pet name.

'I love it here. I always did. But I wanted a different way.'

He resumed walking, Lawrie kept pace with him, wishing she was wearing flatter, sturdier shoes. He had a fast, firm tread; she had always liked that. Hugo was more of a dawdler, and it had driven her mad —as had his admonishments to 'Slow down…it's not a race'.

Jonas didn't look at her as she reached his side but continued as if there hadn't been any break in the conversation. It was as if he was glad he had the chance to explain. And why shouldn't he be? The boy had done well. *Very* well. He hadn't needed her at all. It must be *satisfying* to be in his position. Successful, in control, magnanimously helping out your ex.

Lawrie clenched her fist, digging her nails deep into the palm of her hand. This wasn't how her life, her return to Trengath, was supposed to have been.

'By the time my father had his second heart attack I'd managed to expand the Boat House into twenty-seven seaside locations in the South-West and people were buying into the whole experience—branded T-shirts, mugs, beach towels. So, from a business point of view, expanding the dining experience into a holiday experience made sense.'

Lawrie pulled her mind away from her introspection. Self-pity had never been her style anyway. It didn't get you anywhere.

'I guess,' she said slightly doubtfully. 'But I don't go to my favourite coffee shop and think what this place needs is somewhere for me to sleep.'

'But your favourite coffee shop is near where you live or work,' he pointed out. 'Sure, we're popular with the local population, but in summer especially seventy per cent of our customers are tourists—even if just a small percentage of those people want to take the experience further and holiday with us then that's already a good deal of our marketing done.'

She looked at him in fascination. He sounded like one of her clients.

'I was writing the dissertation for my MBA on brand expansion at the time. Fascinating to put the theory into practice.'

An MBA? Not bad for a boy who'd left school at sixteen. Not that she hadn't known he was capable of so much more. But, truly, had she ever thought him capable of all this? Shame crept over her, hot and uncomfortable. Maybe he was right. She *had* underestimated him.

He flashed her a smile, warm and confiding— a smile that evoked memories of long late-night conversations, of dreams shared, plans discussed. Had she and Hugo ever talked like that? If they had, she couldn't remember.

'Luckily I had been planning what I would do with this place if I were in charge since I was a kid. I've left the hotel itself as pretty high-end, with the rooms still aimed at the luxury end of the market, but I've utilised the woods and the golf course more effectively and I began to reap the rewards almost straight away.'

They were near the top of the small hill. He reached it first and paused, waiting for her to catch up, an expectant look on his face.

She looked down and gasped. 'What on earth...?'

Set beneath them were the woods, which opened almost immediately into a large glade, easily seen from the top of the bank on which they were standing. Inside the glade were eight round white cotton objects that looked a little like mini circus tents.

'Glamping' he said, his voice serious. His eyes, however, had warmed up and were sparkling with amusement at her expression. 'Oh, come on—you're a city girl. Isn't this how the London middle classes enjoy the great outdoors?'

She found her voice. 'You've put *tents* into the woods? Do your parents know? Your dad will have a third heart attack if he sees this.'

'Ah, but these are luxurious, fully catered tents,' he assured her. 'Perfectly respectable. People can enjoy all the hotel facilities, including their own bathrooms and food in the hotel—although there are barbecues if they want to be pioneer types.

They arrive to fully made-up camp beds, there's space to hang clothes, armchairs, rugs, heating. Not what I call camping, but it's hugely popular. The traditional bring-your-own-tent-type campers are on what used to be the golf course, and there are lots of shower and toilet blocks for their use there. According to one review site they are the best camping loos in Cornwall.'

'Well, *there's* an accolade.'

'I'm hoping for a certificate.'

'Anything else?' she asked. 'Tree houses? Yurts? A cave with hot and cold water laid on?'

He chuckled softly, and the sound went straight to the pit of her stomach.

'Just a few stationary camper vans dotted around here and there.'

'Of course there are.' She nodded.

He looked at her, his blue eyes darkening, suddenly intense. 'They're very popular with honeymooners—complete privacy.'

She felt her breath catch as she looked at him, and a shiver goosed its way down her spine. 'A bit cramped,' she said, hearing the husky tone in her voice and hating herself for it.

'They're customised cosy getaways for two—

big beds, good sheets and baskets of food de-
livered.'

'You've thought of everything.'

So different from the two of them, with a
sleeping bag and a couple of blankets, a bottle
of champagne, the moon, the stars, the sound
of the surf. And each other—always each other.
Bodies coiled together, lips, hands, caresses…
She swallowed. How did these memories, buried
so deep, resurface every time this man spoke?

'I had long enough to plan it, watching my parents cater for rich idiots who didn't give a damn
where they were,' he said, his mood changing
instantly from dangerously reminiscent to businesslike again. 'This place is so beautiful, and yet
only a handful of people ever had the opportunity
to enjoy it—and once they were here they had no
idea what was outside the estate walls. Opening
it up to campers and glampers means anyone can
come here, whatever their budget. We make sure
they have all the information they need to go out
and explore, hire them bikes, provide transport.
All our food is sourced locally, and we recruit
and promote locally whenever possible.'

Lawrie laughed, shaking her head in disbelief.

'It's inspired,' she said honestly. 'Utterly inspired, Jonas.'

Without thinking, without even realising what she was doing, she put a hand on his arm, squeezed softly.

'Amazing.'

The feel of his arm was warm and firm under her hand, and the fine cotton of his shirt bunched up under her fingers. How many times had she slid her hand up this arm, admired the strength inherent in the toned muscles as he emerged, sleek and shiny, from the sea? Felt their gentleness as he pulled her in close, encircling her in the safety of his embrace?

'I'm glad you like it.'

Jonas stepped back. Stepped away from her hand, her touch.

'The hotel isn't just the base for the festival—it sets the tone. It's important you understand that. Shall we?'

He gestured back towards the hotel. She shivered, suddenly cold despite the balmy warmth of the day and the wool of her suit jacket. If only she was still with Hugo. If only she were secure in her job. Then seeing Jonas, speaking to him, would have meant nothing apart from a certain nostalgic curiosity. She was feeling vulnerable, that was all.

'You're right—this is the perfect setting for the festival. I see how it works now.' She could do businesslike as well. She'd practically invented it.

He registered the change, a querying eyebrow shooting up as she adjusted her jacket again, smoothing her hair back away from her face, plastering a determinedly polite smile onto her face.

'So, what other changes have you made?' Lawrie kept up a flow of light conversation as Jonas led the way back to the hotel, barely knowing what she was saying, what his answers were.

Thoughts tumbled around her brain. Coming back wasn't easy, starting again was hard, but she had expected that. What she *hadn't* expected, she admitted honestly to herself, was that anything would have changed.

Walking back into Gran's cottage had been like entering a time warp, and for the first couple of days as she'd holed herself up and licked her wounds it had looked as if Trengarth had stayed the same as well.

She had walked down to the harbour on her birthday looking for the safety and comfort of her past. She had truly expected to see the Boat House in its original incarnation—Jonas behind the bar, a little older, a little more thick-set, his mind firmly fixed on waves, on guitar chords, on fun.

She had wanted to validate her choices. To know that even if her present was looking a little shaky at least her past choices had been right. She had been so convinced, once, that Jonas was holding her back, but what if she had been the one holding *him* back?

He was obviously better off without her. Which was *good*, she told herself defiantly, because despite everything she was definitely better off without him.

Or she would be once she had decided exactly what she was going to do.

The familiar niggle of worry gnawed away at her. She had just a few weeks left of her gardening leave—just a few weeks to get a job so much better than her old one that to the outsider it would look like a planned move. Just a few weeks to show Hugo and the senior partners that she was better than their firm. Just a few weeks to get her plan back on track.

They had reached the front of the hotel again and she turned to face Jonas, her features deliberately smooth, matching his. 'This has been fascinating, Jonas, and I can't wait to get started. If you show me where I am to work I'll get set up.'

And then Jonas smiled. A slow, intimate, knowing smile. A smile that said he knew exactly what she was doing. A smile that saw right through her mask. It crinkled the corners of his eyes, drew her gaze to firm lips, to the faint shadow on the sculpted jawline.

It was the kind of smile that offered comfort, acceptance. The kind of smile that invited a girl to lean in, to allow those broad shoulders to take the strain.

It was almost irresistible.

But Lawrie Bennett was made of sterner stuff. Just.

She straightened her shoulders, met his eyes with a challenge. 'After all, you must have a lot to be getting on with.'

The smile deepened. 'Good to see work is still your priority, Lawrie.'

It was. And it evidently was a priority for him as well. So why did he sound so amused?

'The staff entrance is round the back, but you can use the front doors. Just this once.'

Once again Lawrie was following Jonas, moving behind the stylish reception desk and through a door that led to the offices, kitchens and staff bedrooms.

'I have an office here, of course,' he said. 'But I do prefer to work at the Boat House—whether it's because I designed the office there, or because it's where this all began I don't know.' He shrugged. 'A business psychologist would probably have a field-day, trying to work it all out, but I'm not sure I need to know as long as it works and the business keeps growing.'

'You don't live in your parents' apartment?'

He looked surprised at the question. 'Oh, heavens, no. This place needs a whole team of managers and some of them live in. The general manager and his family have the apartment. I bought a place on the seafront a few years ago. One of the old fishermen's cottages by the harbour. You'd like it.'

She nodded, maintaining her cool, interested

air even as a stab of pain shot through her. It had always been her ambition to own one of the stone-built cottages clustered around the harbour. On moonlit nights she and Jonas had strolled along, hands entwined, as she'd pointed out her favourites, and they had laughingly argued over decorating plans, colour schemes, furniture.

Now he lived in one of those cottages, without her.

It was ridiculous to feel wounded. To feel *anything*. After all she had spent the last five years living in a beautiful flat with another man; very soon she fully intended to be in an apartment of her own somewhere completely new. Yet the thought of Jonas living in the dream house of their youth filled her with a wistfulness so intense she could barely catch her breath.

He had opened a door to an empty office and held it open, motioning her to move inside. Swallowing back the unexpected emotion as she went through, she saw the office was a large room, distinguished by two big sash windows, each with a cushioned window seat, and furnished with a large desk, a small meeting table and a sofa.

'This is supposed to be my office,' he explained. 'I never use it, though, so you may as well have it while you're here. As I said, it'll be useful for you to be based on site. I'm sure it's all in your notes, but the hotel itself usually hosts the bands, VIPs and essential staff, and most festival- goers camp in the grounds—although quite a lot book out the local B&Bs and caravan parks too.'

She nodded. Of course she had read all this yesterday, but it was still hard for her to comprehend.

Jonas had started this festival during her first year at Oxford, getting local rock and folk bands to play on the beach for free, raising money for a surfing charity that campaigned against marine and beach pollution. The first ever festival had been a one-night affair and the festival-goers had slept on the beach…if they'd slept at all. Food had, of course, been provided by the Boat House. Lawrie was supposed to have returned to Cornwall for it, but at the last minute had decided to stay in London, where she'd been interning for the summer.

Her refusal to promise that she would attend the third festival had led to the final argument in their increasingly volatile relationship. She had packed her bags on the eve of her twenty-first birthday and gone to London for another summer of interning. At the end of that summer she had returned to Oxford for her fourth and final year. She had never returned to Cornwall.

Not until a week ago.

And now that little beach festival had grown—just like the Boat House, just like Jonas's business. Everything was so much bigger, so different from the small, comforting life she remembered. Three nights, thirty-six bands, family activities, thousands of festival-goers, raising substantial funds for charity—yet still local, still focussed on the best of Cornish music, food, literature. It was daunting.

Not that she was going to confess that to the imposing man standing before her.

Lawrie had never admitted that she needed help before. She wasn't going to start now.

'This is great, Jonas,' she said. 'I can take it from here.'

His mouth quirked. 'I have complete faith in you,' he assured her. 'You know where I am if you need me.'

She nodded, but her mind was completely made up. She did not, *would* not need Jonas Jones. She was going to do this alone. Just as she always did.

CHAPTER FIVE

JONAS LOVED THIS drive. The winding lanes, the glimpses of sea through the dense green hedge-rows. If he put the top down he could smell the intoxicating scent of sweet grass and gorse, feel the sea breeze ruffling his hair.

And he loved the destination. The hotel *he* owned. The hotel *he* had bought. The hotel where his ex-wife was right this moment sitting at his desk, taking care of his festival.

It had been an unexpected couple of days. Of course the village gossips were having a field-day. Again. What would they do without him? He should start charging a licence fee for the resurrection of their favourite soap opera. He would always be that no-good boy who'd broken his parents' hearts, and she would always be the no-better-than-she-should-be teen bride, flighty daughter of a flighty mother. Their roles had been set in stone long before no matter how they tried to redefine them.

Well, the viewers were doomed to disappointment. Reunion episodes were always a let-down. He had no intention of allowing this one to be any different.

Pulling into the gates of the hotel, he felt the usual spark of pride, of ownership, zing through him. Who would have thought the prodigal son would return in such style?

It would be nice, though—just once—to drive through the gates and not be assailed by memories. By the disapproving voices of his parents and their disappointed expectations.

When he'd failed his exams at sixteen his parents had wanted to send him away to boarding school—ostensibly to do retakes, in reality to get him away from his friends. It showed a lack of character, they'd thought, that rather than befriend the other boys from the private school they'd sent him to he preferred to hang around with the village kids.

His hands tightened on the steering wheel. Yes, he probably should have studied rather than sneaking out to swim and surf. Taken some interest in his exams. But his achievements—his interest in food, his surfing skill, his hard-won A* in Design and Technology—had meant nothing. His father couldn't, or wouldn't, boast about his son's perfect dovetailed joints on the golf course.

His parents hadn't ever lost their tempers with him. Cold silence had been their weapon of choice. There had been weeks, growing up, when he could swear they hadn't addressed one word to him. But they'd come close to exploding when Jonas had refused to go to the carefully selected crammer they had found.

Some parents would have been proud, Jonas thought with the same, tired old stab of pain, proud that their child wanted to follow in their footsteps. He had thought his plan was a winner—that he would finally see some approval in their uninterested faces.

He'd been so keyed up when he'd told them his idea to run a café-bar on the hotel's small beach. One that was aimed at locals as well as tourists.

He had even offered to do a few retakes at the local college before studying Hospitality and Tourism.

It hadn't been enough. Nothing he did ever was.

In the end they had reached a grudging compromise. They'd given him the old boat house they hadn't used, preferring to keep their guests—and their guests' wallets—on the hotel grounds, and they'd cut him loose. Set him free.

They'd expected him to fail. To come back, cap in hand, begging for their forgiveness.

Instead, twelve years later, he'd bought them out.

And it had been every bit as satisfying as he had thought it would be. It still was.

And, truth be told, Jonas thought as he swung his car into the staff car park, it was quite satisfying having Lawrie here as well. Working for him once again. Seeing just how much he had accomplished. Just how little he needed her.

Whereas she definitely needed him. She was doing her best to hide it, but he could tell. Her very appearance in Trengarth. Her acceptance of the job. None of it was planned.

And Lawrie Bennett didn't *do* spontaneous.

There were just too many ghosts, and Jonas felt uncharacteristically grim as he walked through the foyer—although he did his best to hide it, playing the jovial host, the approachable boss. If growing up in a hotel, then running a café at sixteen, had taught him anything it was how to put on a mask. Nobody cared about the guy pouring the coffee—about his day or his feelings. They just wanted a drink, a smile and some easy chat. Funny how he had always accused Lawrie of hiding her feelings. In some ways they were exactly the same.

Walking along the carpeted corridor that led to his office—now Lawrie's—he felt a sense of *déjà vu* overwhelm him. Once this had been his father's domain. He had never been welcome here—summoned only to be scolded. Even stripping out the heavy mahogany furniture and redecorating it hadn't changed the oppressive feeling. No wonder he preferred to base himself at the harbour.

He paused at the shut door. He didn't usually knock at his employees' doors, but then again they weren't usually shut. And this was *his* office, after all. Jonas felt his jaw clench tight. Nothing was simple when Lawrie was involved—not even going through his own damn door in his own damn hotel.

He twisted the heavy brass door and swung it

open with more force than necessary, striding into the room.

Then he stopped. Blinked in surprise.

'You've certainly made yourself at home.'

There was a small overnight bag open on the floor. Clothes were strewn on the table, chairs and across the sofa—far more clothes than could ever possibly fit into such a small case. Jeans, tops, dresses, skirts—all a far cry from the exquisitely tailored suits and accessories that in just two days Lawrie was already famous for wearing to work.

If Jonas had to hear one more awed conversation discussing whether she wore couture, high-end High Street or had a personal tailor, then he would make all his staff—no matter what their job—adopt the waiting staff's uniform of bright blue Boat House logo tee and black trousers.

Lawrie was on the floor, pulling clothes out of the bag with a harassed expression on her face.

'Have you moved in?' he asked as politely as he could manage, whilst making no attempt to keep the smirk from his face.

Lawrie looked up, her face harassed, her hair falling out of what had once, knowing Lawrie,

been a neat bun. She pushed a tendril of the dark
silky stuff back behind an ear and glared at him.
'Don't you knock?'

'Not usually. Are you going somewhere?'

'Road trip,' she said tersely. 'And I have nothing to wear.'

Jonas raised an eyebrow and looked pointedly
at the sofa. And at the table. Finally, slowly, he
allowed his gaze to linger on the floor. A pair of
silky lilac knickers caught his eye and held it for
one overlong second before he pulled his gaze
reluctantly away.

'Half this stuff is mine. Only it's about fifteen
years old—whatever I still had at Gran's. The
rest is Fliss's, and as we aren't the same height or
size it's not really much use. The truth is I don't
really know how to dress down. Where I live it's
all skinny jeans and caramel knee-length boots,
with cashmere for shopping and lunch or yoga
pants at home. None of that is very suitable at
all,' she finished, with a kind of wail.

'Suitable for what?' Jonas decided not to ask
why she was packing here and not at home. He
wasn't sure she even knew.

'The road trip,' she said.

He cocked an enquiring eyebrow and she rocked back on her heels and sighed. Irritably.

'*You* know! Suzy always gets a couple of local bands to come and play Wave Fest. They send in their CDs, or links to their downloads or whatever, and she whittles them down to a shortlist and then goes to see them play live. At a *gig*,' she said, pronouncing the word 'gig' with an odd mixture of disdain and excitement. 'I haven't been to a gig in years,' she added.

'Not much call for yoga pants at Cornish gigs.'

'Or cashmere,' Lawrie agreed, missing his sarcasm completely, or just ignoring it. 'Three of the shortlisted bands are playing over the next three nights so I'm going to see them all. Two of them are in the county, but tomorrow's gig is in Devon, so it made sense to plan a whole trip and do some mystery shopping at some of the caterers and cafés we've got tendering as well. We're behind in letting them know. Only that means a three-day trip and I don't have anything to wear. Why do you have to be so inclusive and get other people to provide the food?' she ended bitterly.

'Because we couldn't possibly feed thousands of people, and it's good publicity to make the festival a celebration of local food as well,' Jonas said, his mouth twitching at Lawrie's woebegone expression.

She looked like somebody being dragged to a three-day conference on dental drills—not like someone heading out for a long weekend of music and food, all on expenses.

He took pity on her.

'Right, unfortunately packing light may not be an option,' Jonas said, gesturing to the small bag. 'Three gigs in three nights? You'll need to be prepared for beer-spills,' he clarified at her enquiring expression.

Lawrie pulled a face. 'I'm not planning to *mosh*.'

'You did once.'

Lightly said but the words evoked a torrent of memories. Lawrie, so small and slight. Vulnerable. Hurling herself into the mass of bodies right at the front of the stage. It had taken him a long time to make his way through the tightly packed, sweaty mass to find her, jumping ecstatically to the beat of the music, eyes half closed. He'd liked staying near her, to protect her from the crush as the crowd moved to the music.

Lawrie's eyebrow furrowed. 'What did I wear?'

He looked at her incredulously. 'How am I supposed to remember? Probably jeans…' A memory hit him, of thin straps falling off tanned shoulders, a glimpse of skin at the small of her back. 'And a top?' he added. 'Was there a green one?'

Her eyes lit up. 'Hang on!' She jumped up and ran over to the table, where she sifted through a pile of brightly coloured tops. 'Do you remember this?' She held up a light green floaty top.

Jonas wouldn't have said he was a particularly observant man, especially when it came to clothes. His last girlfriend had claimed that he said, 'You look nice…' on autopilot. And it was true that he generally didn't notice haircuts or new outfits. He knew better than to admit it, but he preferred his women laid-back and practical. Jeans, trainers, a top. Even a fleece if they were out walking. There was nothing less sexy than a woman stumbling along the clifftops in unsuitable shoes and shivering because her most flattering jacket proved useless against a chill sea breeze.

But the sight of that green top took his breath away, evoking the beat of a drum, the smell of mingled beer, sweat and cigarettes in the air. Not the most pleasant of smells, yet in the back room of a pub, a club or a town hall, as guitars wailed and people danced, it fitted. Dark, dirty, hot. The feel of Lawrie pressed against him in the fast-moving, mesmerised crowd.

He swallowed. 'I think so,' he managed to say, as normally as he could.

Lawrie regarded it doubtfully. 'I guess it will fit. I'm the same size, and luckily Gran had them all laundered.' Now it was her turn to swallow, with a glint in her eye.

Had she grieved properly for her gran? For the woman who'd brought her up? The woman who had provided him with a sanctuary, a sympathetic shoulder and a lot of sound advice?

Had helped him become the man he was today.

'There you go, then,' he said. 'Three tops like that, some jeans for the gigs, something similar for the day, and pyjamas. Easy.' He tried not to look at the lilac silk knickers. 'Plus essentials. Where are you staying?'

'I'm not sure. Fliss was supposed to have sorted out accommodation. Wherever I can get in last-minute, I guess.'

She didn't look particularly enthusiastic and he didn't blame her. Three nights alone in anonymous, bland rooms didn't sound like much fun.

'I'm looking into buying a small chain that covers the whole of the South-West,' he said. 'We could see if any of those are near where you need to be and you can do some evaluation while you're there. Let me know what you think of them.'

She nodded. 'I'm near Liskeard tonight, then over to Totnes tomorrow, and back towards Newquay on Saturday. I could drive straight back from there, but there are several food producers I want to sample around that area so it makes sense to stay over.' Her eyes darkened. 'I wish Fliss hadn't bailed, though. It would be nice to have a second opinion.'

'Isn't she going with you?'

'She was supposed to be—we were going to road-trip. Like Thelma and Louise—only without guns or Brad Pitt. But Dave has tickets for some play she really wanted to see and I think he wants to make a weekend of it. It's fine. I'm quite capable. Only she was going to sort out the accommodation and didn't get round to it.'

Her face said exactly what she thought of such woeful disorganisation.

Jonas suppressed a chuckle. He'd have liked to see them set off—Fliss laid-back and happy to wing it, Lawrie clutching a schedule and a stopwatch. 'I'll have a word with Alex and get him to find you some appropriate rooms. What time are you off?'

'After lunch, I think. If I can get packed by then.' She cast a despairing look at the clothes-strewn room.

'I'll let you know what Alex says. Let him arrange your bookings—he knows all the good places. That's why I employ him.'

'Thanks.' She was trying to hide it, but there was still uncertainty, worry in the dark eyes.

'No need to thank me; it's his job. I'll see you later.'

Jonas needed some air. The room suddenly felt hot, claustrophobic. He'd been working too hard, that was the problem. Head down, losing himself in spreadsheets and figures and meetings. He hadn't been near a board for days, hadn't touched a guitar.

He needed a break. Lucky Lawrie. A road trip sounded perfect.

Good food, music, and some time on the road. It really *did* sound perfect.

If only he had known earlier he could have offered to go instead. A trip was just what the doctor had ordered.

Lawrie checked her watch. Again. This was ridiculous. She had planned to be on the road fifteen minutes ago. Nothing was more irritating than being behind schedule.

Even worse, she was hungry. It must be the Cornish air, because far from acting like a normal jilted bride, and existing on tears alone, for the first time in years Lawrie had a real appetite. Every day she went to the staff dining room promising herself she would just have the soup. A *small* bowl of soup. Because she strongly suspected it was made with double cream.

Yet every day she would find herself drifting over to the bread. Carbs, wheat, gluten. Things that Lawrie had been depriving herself of for so long she had completely forgotten why. Bread covered with real butter, with rich, creamy cheese…sharp, tangy cheese. Even worse, she sometimes had crisps on the side, and the handful of lettuce and tomatoes she added to her heaped plate went no way to assuaging her guilt.

Only—as the pang in her stomach reminded her all too well—she was skipping lunch today. The first stop on her schedule was a baker's, and she had an Indian restaurant and an ice cream maker to fit in today. She might be the same size as her teen self right now but, she thought, the chances of her remaining that slender were looking very, very slim.

She checked her watch again and shook her head. She couldn't wait. Her schedule was packed. Alex would just have to leave her a message and let her know where she would be staying that night. She swallowed. That was okay. He would hardly leave her to sleep in the car. So what if she hadn't checked out the hotel website and printed out directions in case the sat nav didn't work? This was a road trip, not a military manoeuvre.

Lawrie grabbed her handbag and moved towards the door, picking up the stuffed overnight bag and the shopper she had quickly bought in the hotel shop to carry the overspill as she did so. She averted her eyes from the mass of clothes on the sofa. She had tried to tidy up but it still looked as if a whole class of fifteen-year-olds had done a clothes-swap in the normally tidy office.

'Okay, then,' she said out loud, but the words sounded flat in the empty room and her stomach lurched with the all too familiar panic she'd been trying to hide since Fliss had pulled out last night.

Lawrie was no stranger to travelling alone, to making decisions alone, but usually she was clothed with the confidence of her profession. Sharp suits, intimidating jargon, business class flights. This time it would just be Lawrie Bennett, unemployed and jilted. Alone.

She dropped her bags, pressing a fist to her stomach, trying to quell the churning inside. For goodness' sake, she dealt with CEOs all the time. How could standing in a dark room listening to music be scarier than walking into a hostile boardroom?

But it was.

It had been so long. Gigging belonged to a younger, more naive Lawrie. A Lawrie she had said goodbye to many years before. Still, she thought grimly, it would all make an amusing anecdote one day—possibly even at a job interview. An example of how she was prepared to go the extra mile.

The trill of her desk phone made her jump. Good—Alex at last. Walking over to it, she prayed for a reprieve. There were no hotel rooms left in the whole of Cornwall.... She was needed elsewhere...

'Sorted out your sartorial crisis?'

Not Alex. Warm, comforting tones, as caressing as a hot bath on a cold night. A voice she wanted to confide her fears in—a voice that promised safety. Sanctuary.

'I'm running late,' she said, more sharply than she had intended. The last thing she needed was for Jonas to guess how relieved she was to hear his voice, to know how scared she was. 'Did your guy manage to sort out a place for tonight? I really can't hold on any longer.'

'Everything's organised. Come and meet me in the car park.'

Was that laughter tinting the deep tones? 'Fine. I'm on my way.'

Laden down, it took Lawrie a few minutes to make her way along the corridors and through the staff door that led to the car park.

The weather had cooled suddenly, and the sky was a mixture of grey and white with occasional glimpses of hopeful blue. It meant nothing. Cornwall was full of micro climates, and she had packed for every eventuality bar blizzards.

Her convertible Beetle was tucked away in the far corner of the car park. Hugo had laughed at it—told her that she was obviously still a hippy surf girl at heart—although she had eschewed all the pretty pastel colours for a sensible metallic grey. She had thought of it as the perfect choice for a city car: small and compact. But its rounded lines and cheerful shape fitted in here. Maybe Hugo had been right about that part of her at least.

She pushed Hugo from her mind. He didn't belong here, in this world dominated by the sea and the open country. In the new life she was trying to make for herself. She looked around for Jonas but he wasn't by her car or by the hotel entrance.

'Lawrie?'

There he was, predictably enough standing by

one of the camper vans that were always dotted around the car park, several of them staff vehicles. She was pretty sure ownership of one guaranteed you a job here.

This van was freshly painted a minty green, its contrasting white trim bright. Jonas leant against it, arms folded, one long leg casually crossed over the other, a look of enjoyment on his face. The same feeling of safety she had experienced on the phone rushed over her as she walked towards him.

'I'm behind schedule, so this had better not take long,' she said as she stopped in front of him, dropping her bags at her feet.

She wasn't going to give in to temptation, to allow her eyes to flicker up and down the long, muscled legs, the firm torso that broadened out in exactly the right place. She wasn't going to pause at the neck—what *was* it with this man and his unbuttoned shirts? One button lower and it would look sleazy, but as it was he managed to show just enough chest to tantalise. And she wasn't going to linger on the perfectly defined jawline, on the cheekbones wasted on a mere man—even on this one. She certainly wasn't going to step closer and allow her hand to brush that lock of dirty blond hair back from his forehead, no matter how much her hand ached to.

'You have a schedule?' He shook his head. 'Of course you do. A timetable, printed maps, telephone numbers all printed out. I bet there's a clipboard.'

Hot colour crept over her cheeks. 'There's nothing wrong with being organised.'

He raised an eyebrow in pretend surprise. 'I didn't say there was. It's an excellent quality in a festival-planner and an equally excellent one in a navigator. Come on—hop in.'

Confusion warred with panic and a tiny, unwanted tendril of hope. 'What do you mean?'

Jonas gestured to the van. 'She doesn't know whether to be pleased or offended that you don't recognise her, even though she spent a good six months being restored.'

'They all look the same,' Lawrie replied automatically, but her eyes were searching the camper van, looking for the tell-tale signs, looking for the rust, the dents. 'That's not Bar...? Not your old van?'

'You nearly said her name.' A smirk played

around the firm mouth. 'Not looking so old now, is she? A facelift—well, an everything lift, really—new custom interior, new engine. She's never been in better shape.'

'Boys and their toys,' Lawrie scoffed, but secretly she was impressed.

The old van did look amazing—a total change from the ancient rust bucket whose tattered interior might have been original but had definitely seen better days. The same magic wand that had been waved over the Boat House, over the hotel, even over Jonas himself had been hard at work here.

'She looks good, but I still don't get what that has to do with me.'

The blue eyes gleamed. 'You said yourself you needed a second opinion.'

The tiny tendril of hope grew larger, bloomed. Lawrie stamped down on it. Hard. 'I said Fliss was going to *give* me a second opinion—not that I needed one.'

'And I realised that I need to recharge my batteries.'

He carried on as if she hadn't spoken, pushing himself away from the van and sauntering slowly towards her. Lawrie fought an instinctive urge to take a step back. With his unhurried grace he reminded her of a predator, blue eyes fixed on her, hypnotic.

Lawrie swallowed, her mouth suddenly dry, her heart pounding so loudly she was sure he could hear it. 'I'm not sure it's a good idea. Working together is one thing, but spending time alone after everything…' Her voice trailed off. Lost for words again. It was becoming a habit around him.

Jonas paused in his tracks. 'But we *will* be working. Second opinions, remember?'

'Alone—we'll be working together alone,' she snapped.

He quirked an eyebrow. 'Oh, I'm sorry. I totally misread the situation. I thought you were totally over me, what with the divorce and the fiancé and the nine years apart, but if this is awkward for you maybe I had better keep my distance.'

He stood grinning at her. He obviously thought he had the upper hand.

Lawrie could feel her teeth grinding together. With a huge effort she unclenched her jaw, forcing a smile onto her face. 'I hate to burst your highly inflated opinion of yourself,' she said, as sweetly as she could, 'but I was only thinking of you. If this isn't awkward for you, then great— by all means join me.'

He moved a step closer, so close they were nearly touching. She could see the smattering of freckles that dusted the bridge of his nose, the tops of his cheeks. They gave him a boyish air, emphasised by the hair falling over his forehead, the impish grin.

But he was no boy. Jonas Jones was all grown up.

'Ready?' he asked, eyes locked on hers.

She stared straight back at him, channelling every ounce of cool professionalism she had right back at him. 'Of course.'

'Then let's go.'

'Did Alex book the hotels? I can plot out the best routes for the entire weekend once I know where we're staying.'

Jonas had to hand it to her. Lawrie was never knocked down for long. He could have sworn that his decision to crash her trip had completely thrown her but she was hiding it well. The road atlas open on her lap, clipboard and pen in hand, she was seemingly back in control.

For now.

Of course she had a point. A very good point. Spending three days on the road with any colleague would be testing. Make that colleague the person you'd once thought was the love of your life and things got a little more difficult.

But this was purely business. Lawrie had been thrown in at the deep end, after all. She might be a whizz with a spreadsheet and able to decipher the finer points of contracts in the blink of an eye, but Jonas was prepared to bet good money that she hadn't been anywhere near a tent or a crowded gig in years. This was his festival—his reputation at stake. He might agree that in the circumstances Lawrie was the right person to help them out, but she still needed hand-holding. Metaphorically, of course.

Of course he *might* be playing with fire. But what was life without a little danger? He'd been playing it safe for far too long.

Time to light the fireworks.

Jonas nodded towards a folder on the dashboard. 'Our accommodation is in there.'

Concealing a smile, Jonas watched out of the corner of his eye as she slid the folder onto her knee and pulled out the sheaf of paper from inside.

Her brow crinkled. 'These aren't hotels.'

'Excellent opportunity to check out some of the competition,' he said.

'You own a hotel.'

'And a campsite,' he reminded her.

'But I'm not set for camping. I don't camp— not any more.' Her voice was rising. 'I don't even own a sleeping bag.'

'Relax,' Jonas said easily. 'I'm not subjecting you to a tent. Barb has everything we need. You won't even need a bag. I have sheets and quilts. Even pillowcases.'

'We're sleeping in *here*? Both of us?'

'She's a four-berther, remember?' He flashed a grin over at her, looking forward to her reaction. 'Do you want to go on top or shall I?'

'I'm not nineteen any more, Jonas.'

Lawrie's face was flushed, her eyes dark with emotion. Anger? Fear? Maybe a combination of both.

'This really isn't acceptable.'

Jonas raised an eyebrow appraisingly. What was she so scared of? 'I'm sorry, Lawrie, I didn't think this would be a big deal. I really do want to see how the facilities at the sites compare with mine. Look, if you feel that strongly about it I can drop you at a motel or a B&B after tonight's gig. But I promise you you'll get a better night's sleep here than in some anonymous hotel chain bedroom.'

'Call me old-fashioned, but I like en-suite facilities.'

But his conciliatory tone seemed to have worked as she sounded more petulant than angry. He decided to push it a little.

'I promise you we won't be roughing it. Barb's newly sprung and very comfortable. All these sites have electric hook-up and plenty of shower blocks. The place I have picked out for tonight has a very well-regarded organic restaurant too. I thought it would be good to compare it with the Boat House. And Saturday's site prides itself on its sea views, which is one thing we're lacking. I really would value your opinion.'

'But I thought you had the best toilets in Cornwall? I won't settle for less.'

Was that a small smile playing around the full mouth?

'If I didn't think every single one of these toilets weren't a serious contender I promise you I wouldn't have dreamt of bringing you along. Come on, Lawrie, it'll be fun. Food, music and the stars. I know I need the break. And...' he slid his eyes over to her again, noting the dark shadows under her eyes, the air of bewildered fragility she wore whenever her professional mask slipped '...I'll bet everything I own that you do too.'

'This isn't a break—this is work,' she reminded him primly.

'True,' he conceded. 'But who's to say we can't have fun while we're working?'

She wound a tendril of hair around her finger, staring out of the window, lost in thought. 'Okay, then,' she said finally. 'I'll give it one night. But if it's cold or uncomfortable or you snore—' she gave him a dark look '—then tomorrow we're in a hotel. Deal?'

'Deal,' he said. 'Okay, then, woman-with-clipboard, which road do you want me to take?'

CHAPTER SIX

'THIS IS SO good.'

'Better than your Pinot Noirs and Sauvignon Blancs?'

Lawrie took a long sip of the cool, tart cider and shook her head. 'Not better—different. I'm not sure I'd want to drink it in a restaurant. Too filling, for a start,' she finished, turning the pint glass full of amber-coloured liquid round in her hands, admiring the way it caught the light.

'They have a micro-brewery on site.' Jonas was reading the tasting cards. 'Rhubarb cider—that sounds intriguing. I wonder if they would want a stall at the festival? Talking of which, have you made a decision on the bands yet?'

Lawrie pulled a face. 'It's so hard,' she said. 'They were all good, and so different. Seriously, how do you compare punk folk with rock with acoustic?' She shook her head. 'Who would have thought punk folk even worked, and yet they were fab. Can I ask them all?'

'You're the organiser; it's up to you,' Jonas said. He gave her a mock stern look. 'Not last night's support, though. We want people to *enjoy* their festival-going experience.'

'Oh, I don't know.' Lawrie smiled at him sweetly. 'I thought the part where she read out poetry to a triangle beat was inspiring. Especially the poem about her menstrual cycle.'

'Stop!' Jonas was covering his ears. 'Those words are seared onto my brain. As is that triangle. I swear I could hear it in my sleep. *Ting, ting ting.*' He shuddered.

Lawrie laughed and took another sip. 'I think the triangle represented her feminine aura.'

It was amazing, how comfortable she was. How comfortable *they* were. Having him around, driving, tasting, listening, bouncing ideas—it had made the whole trip easy, fun. And it hadn't been awkward. Well, hardly at all. Lying in the upper berth listening to his deep breathing had been a little *odd*. A little lonely, maybe. But nothing she couldn't shake off.

And he'd been a perfect gentleman. Which was good, obviously.

'It was a good idea of yours to stay an extra night,' she said with a small, happy sigh.

Jonas had been right about the views. The final campsite was perfectly placed in the dip of a valley, with the beach and sea clearly visible from their sheltered pitch. Lawrie wriggled back in her chair and closed her eyes, savouring the feel of the late-afternoon sun on her face.

'It seemed a shame to get a pitch with these views and then not be around to enjoy them,' Jonas said. 'Besides, we deserve some relaxation. And we discovered this cider.' He held up his pint with a satisfied smile. 'And that crêperie this morning. I think you should consider that patisserie too—their croissant was a work of art.'

'Hmm…' Lawrie opened her eyes and reached down to the folder at her feet. Picking it up, she flicked through it thoughtfully. 'They were good, weren't they? And the bakers near Liskeard were superb. I think that's enough pastries and bread though, don't you? We need some diversity. Two ice cream suppliers, four breweries, one Indian, one Thai and an Indonesian takeaway. Paella, the baked potato stall...'

'Stop right there.'

Jonas held his hand up and, startled, Lawrie let the folder slip shut.

'Lawrie Bennett, it is Sunday afternoon. You have been working day and night all weekend. Relax, enjoy the view, and drink your cider.'

A warm glow spread through her at his words. Nobody else had ever cared about how hard she worked, told her to slow down. She needed it. Somehow, when brakes were being handed out Lawrie had been last in line.

They lay side by side, sprawled out in the deck-chairs, united in a companionable silence. That was another thing, she thought drowsily. He was easy to talk to but she didn't *have* to talk to him, to entertain. She was free to be lost in her own head if she wanted.

It was nice to be sitting here with no plans, nothing to tick off on her physical or mental to-do list. It was just... Lawrie shifted in her seat. What were they going to do tonight? At least her sched-ule had meant there were no awkward gaps to be filled. Their conversation had revolved around the food they were tasting, the music they were listening to. But tonight stretched ahead—empty. Maybe there was another band playing locally. Or another restaurant to check out. A seafood stall might be an interesting addition to the mix.

'Stop it.'

Lawrie turned her head in surprise. 'Stop what?'

'Timetabling the evening.'

How did he know? 'I'm not,' she said. Then, a little more truthfully, 'I was just thinking about later. Wondering what we were going to do.'

'We haven't stopped for three days,' Jonas pointed out. 'Do we have to do anything?'

'No...' she said doubtfully. 'Only what about food? Or when it gets dark? Not that I'm not enjoying the sun and the view, but it will start to cool off in an hour or so.'

'Good thing we packed jumpers, then.'

The teasing tone was back in his voice and Lawrie squirmed, hot with embarrassment. It was unfair of him to make her feel uptight. Just because she liked to know what was coming next. Hugo had liked her organisational skills. Maybe that was what had attracted him to his secretary?

Not the leopard print thong but the way she organised his diary.

'Okay.'

Jonas was sitting up in his chair and she could feel his eyes fixed on her, despite the sunglasses shielding them.

'I haven't made notes *or* a list, and I don't own a clipboard, but I had vaguely thought of a walk, finishing up at the farm shop for cheese and bread and more of this excellent cider. Then back to the van, where I can finally take cold-blooded, nine-year-old revenge for *quilling* on a triple word score. If you're up to the challenge, that is?'

That sounded really pleasant. In fact it sounded perfect. Almost dangerously so.

'Misplaced confidence was always your problem,' Lawrie said, adjusting her own sunglasses, hoping he couldn't see just how much the evening he had outlined appealed to her. 'There have been many high-scoring words since then, Mr Jones. But if you are willing to risk your pride again, I am more than willing to take you down.'

Jonas leant forward, so close his face was almost touching hers, his breath sweet on her cheek. 'I look forward to it.'

'That is *not* a word!'

'It is.' Lawrie couldn't hide the beam on her face. Ah, the sweet smell of victory. 'Check the dictionary.'

'I don't care what the dictionary says,' Jonas argued. 'Use it in a coherent sentence.'

Foolish, foolish boy. He should know better than to challenge Lawrie Bennett at Scrabble. Or at any game.

'How many *exahertz* are these gamma rays?' she said, sitting back and enjoying his reaction.

'You have never, ever used that sentence in your whole life!'

'No,' she conceded. 'But I could. If I went to work at CERN, for instance, or had a physics laboratory as a client. Besides, the rules don't specify that you have to have used the word in everyday conversation.'

'They should do,' Jonas grumbled, staring at the board in some dismay.

As he should, she thought, looking at the scores neatly written down on the pad in front of her.

There was no way he could win now. And if she could just prevent him from narrowing the gap too much…a two-hundred-point lead was so satisfying.

Leaning back against the bench, she began to add up her points. They were both sitting on the floor of the camper van, the amost full board between them. The van doors were slid fully open, giving the scene a dramatic backdrop as the sun sank into the sea, leaving a fiery path on the top of the calm waves.

'That is thirty-one tripled, plus fifty for getting all my letters out. It's a shame it's the H on the double letter score, but all in all not a bad round. Okay, your turn.'

'I don't think I want to play any more,' Jonas said, disgust on his face as he surveyed his letter tiles. 'Not even *you* could manage to make a word out of three Is, a U, two Os and an R.'

Lawrie bit back a smile as she surveyed the board. 'Oh, dear,' she said, keeping her face completely serious. 'I think the official Scrabble term for your situation is screwed. *Ow!* What was that for?'

'Excessive smugness.' Jonas held up a second cushion. 'Don't think I won't,' he threatened.

Retrieving the cushion he'd already lobbed in her direction, Lawrie held it up in front of her, half shield, half offensive weapon. 'You just try it, Jones.'

He eyed her. 'A challenge? Really, Lawrie? You may, on this occasion, have won on brains, but I am always going to win on brawn.'

'Brawn,' she scoffed, uneasily aware of a tightening in her abdomen—a kind of delicious apprehension uncoiling—as she brandished her pillow. 'At your age?'

'In the prime of my life,' he said. 'Never been in better shape. What?' He laughed indignantly as Lawrie collapsed into giggles. 'It's true.'

'Says the man sat on a caravan floor, unshaven and holding a cushion!' It was hard to get the words out.

'It's not a caravan, you blasphemer. This is a classic and you know it. Besides, *you* can't talk. If only all your fashion admirers could see you now they would be totally disappointed. Nothing chic about leggings and a sweatshirt—even I know that.'

Swallowing back the laughter, Lawrie hugged her knees to her chest. 'Yoga pants and cashmere, actually.'

It felt good to laugh. Free.

Trying hard not to think about how long it had been since she had laughed like that, Lawrie fastened onto Jonas's last words. 'Hang on—what do you mean, fashion admirers?'

Jonas shook his head and pushed the Scrabble board away, sliding down so only his head and shoulders were propped up against the bench seat, the rest of his long, lean body sprawled comfortably along the floor.

He took up a lot of room. A lot of air. Lawrie swallowed and adjusted her gaze so that she was looking straight ahead, at the glorious sunset, at fresh air. Not at the denim-clad legs lying close to her. Close enough to touch.

'I dress really conservatively for work,' she said, probing for an answer as Jonas seemed disinclined to speak. 'And my only night out was on my birthday.'

'Apparently West London's "conservative" is Trengarth's cutting edge,' Jonas said, swirling the Scrabble tiles around on the board and mixing up the words. 'It's all about the cut, or so I've heard. Definitely not High Street, they say.'

'I *do* get my suits made for me by a tailor who specialises in women's clothes.' Why did it feel like an admission of guilt? 'They fit better, though I wouldn't call them fashionable. But I don't know why I am explaining this to you.' She rounded on Jonas. 'If your suits aren't handmade I'll eat a Scrabble tile.'

He grinned, picking up an *I* and holding it out to her. 'Here you go—there are too many of these anyway.' Lawrie raised an eyebrow at him and he palmed the tile. 'Okay, you win. I *do* frequent an establishment in Plymouth run by a gentleman who trained on Savile Row.'

'I knew it!' The moment of triumph was short-lived as the impact of his words hit. Lawrie's chest tightened painfully and she breathed deeply, slowly. 'Why do people care about what I wear?'

Jonas looked surprised. 'They don't—not really. Only you're new, have history with me, and you look smarter than anyone else. It was bound to make a bit of a stir. It's not a big deal.'

But it was. 'I don't like being talked about. No one even noticed my suits in the City. Maybe I should get some new clothes for the rest of the summer.'

'What on earth for?' He sounded incredulous.

A wave of irritation swept over her. 'To blend in. The last thing I want is to be noticed for anything but my work.'

'People aren't exactly staring at you as you walk down the street,' Jonas pointed out. 'Wait...' He pulled his legs in and sat up, facing her. Blue eyes studied her face intently. 'Is this why you were so stressed about what to bring on this trip? You wanted to blend in?'

'There's no reason to sound so judgmental.' Lawrie could feel her face heating up, a prickly and uncomfortable warmth spreading down her neck and chest. 'I'm not comfortable standing out from the crowd. No big deal.'

He was still looking at her. Looking into her, as if he could see her soul. As if he was unsure about what he was seeing there. It took every bit of self-control that she had not to squirm or pull away.

'Is it, Law?' he said softly 'Is it just about blending in?'

'I don't know what you're talking about.' She

wanted to pull away, look away, but it was as if
his eyes had a hypnotic effect on her. She was
paralysed, stuck to the spot, as he stared at her
searchingly.

'You didn't sing in London. Not once in nine
years.'

'For goodness' sake, Jonas, I was busy!'

'What *did* you do? Apart from work.'

She tried to remember but it was all fog. It
seemed like a lifetime ago. 'We had dinner with
friends. Went to the theatre, to museums and exhibitions. The usual things.'

'Usual for who? West London professionals like
you?' His gaze sharpened. 'You're a tribal ani-
mal, aren't you, Lawrie? You like to dress the
part, act the part—whatever that part might be.
What is it you really want? You like? Do you
even know?'

'What do you care?' The words were torn from
her. 'As soon as my life diverged from yours you
gave up on me. So don't you dare be so damn
superior—don't act like I'm letting you down by
trying to fit in.'

'But you're not.' He looked surprised. 'Why
would you be letting me down? But are you let-

ting yourself down, Lawrie? If you spend your whole life hiding your own needs and wants away can you ever be really happy?'

'Happiness is not about *things*.' The words snapped out of her, surprising her with their fierceness, their certainty. 'Clothes, hobbies, food—they're just trappings, Jonas. I don't care about any of them. All I want—all I have ever wanted—is to be successful, to be independent. To stick to the plan.'

'Is this the plan? To be here with me?'

It was like a punch straight to the stomach, winding her with its strength. 'No,' she said after a long pause. 'No, this wasn't in the plan. But I'm adaptable, Jonas. I'm strong. Don't ever mistake a desire to fit in with weakness. Lions blend in with the Sahara, you know.'

He threw his head back and laughed. The sound jarred with her jangled nerves.

'Weak is the last word I'd use to describe you. Lioness, on the other hand...'

It was his turn to duck as she threw a cushion at him.

'I was just agreeing with you,' he protested.

'If you had lived with my mother you'd have

learned to fit in as well,' Lawrie said. She didn't know why she was telling him this—why she needed him to understand. But she did. She needed him to know that she wasn't shallow or weak. 'One moment I'm living in Stockbroker-ville in Surrey, learning French and pony-riding, the next we're in a commune near Glastonbury and my mother is trying to make me answer to the name of Star. She changed completely, de-pending on who she was with, and she never went for the same type twice.'

'I know,' Jonas said, pity softening the keen eyes. 'It was hard for you.'

Lawrie shook her head. 'I don't need you to feel sorry for me. I'm just explaining. What I wore, ate, did, the friends I had—they were in-terchangeable, dependent on her whims. If I had cared, had tried to hang on to *things*, it would have been unbearable. So I kept my head down, I worked hard, and I vowed that I would be so successful that I would never have to be depen-dent on anyone. And I'm not.'

'Is that why you and the fiancé split? Because you didn't need him?'

'No.' Of course it wasn't. Hugo had *liked* her

independence. Hadn't he? 'It was…complicated.' That was one word for it. 'Is that why you wanted out? Because I didn't need *you*?'

'Oh, Lawrie.' There was no lightness in his voice, in his face, at all. 'I was used to that. Not being needed. And, if you remember, in the end you were the one that walked away.'

'Maybe…' Her voice was low. 'Maybe I was afraid that I did need you.'

'Would that have been so bad?' He examined her face, searching for answers behind the mask.

She shook her head and another lock of hair fell out of the loose ponytail, framing her face. 'Bad? It would have been terrible. I was barely started on my path. Oxford, an internship at one of the best City firms… And I seriously, *seriously* considered giving it all up. For you. For a man. Just like my mother would have. Just like she did again and again. I *had* to leave, Jonas.' She turned to him, eyes wide, pleading for understanding. 'I had to hold on to me.'

And in doing so she had let go of him. Jonas closed his eyes for a second, seeing a flash of his heartbroken younger self frozen in time. He hadn't wasted a single emotion on his parents' rejection, pouring all that need, all his love, into the slight girl now sitting beside him. It had been far too much for someone so young to carry.

He reached out and cupped her cheek. Her skin was soft beneath his hand. 'I guess I needed you to choose me. I needed *somebody* to choose me. I still needed validation back then. It was a lot to put on you. Too much.'

'Maybe you were right. We were too young.' Her eyes were filled with sadness and regret. 'I didn't want to agree with you, to prove all the *I told you so* right, but we had a lot of growing up to do. We weren't ready for such a big step.'

He nodded. Suddenly he didn't feel any anger or contempt towards her or towards their shared past. Just an underlying sadness for the idealistic kids they had once been. For their belief that love really was all they needed.

He was still touching her cheek. She leant into him trustingly and he turned his hand to run the back of it down the side of her face, learning once again the angle of her cheekbone, the contours of her chin, the smoothness of her skin.

Jonas had made some rules for himself before

he came on this trip. No talking about the past, no flirting, and definitely, absolutely no touching.

But sometimes rules were meant to be broken.

Slowly, deliberately, he let his fingers trail further down her face, brushing her full mouth before dipping down to her chin. He let them linger there for one long, agonising moment, tilting her face towards him, giving her ample time to pull away, to stop him, before he leant in slowly— oh, so slowly.

It was a butterfly kiss. So light, so brief, their lips barely touching. Jonas pulled back, searching her face for consent. Her eyes were closed, her face angled towards his, lips slightly parted. Expectant. It was all the agreement he needed.

He shifted closer to her, closing the space between them as he slid one arm around her slender shoulders. The other hand moved from her chin to the sweet spot at the nape of her neck. She moved in too—an infinitesimal shift, yet one that brought her body into full contact with his. Her face lifted, waiting, expecting. Jonas looked down at her for one moment—at the face at once so familiar and yet so strange to him, at the dark eyelashes, impossibly long, improbably thick, the creamy skin, the lush, full mouth waiting for him.

And a gentleman should never keep a lady waiting.

Another fleeting kiss, and another, and another. Until, impatient, she moaned and pressed closer in, her mouth opening under his, seeking, wanting. She tasted of cider, of sunshine. She tasted like summer, like coming home, and he deepened the kiss, pulling her even closer until they were pressed together, her arms wound around his neck. His own arms were holding her tightly to him, one bunching the silky strands of her hair, the other caressing the planes of her back through the lightness of her top.

It was like being a teenager again, entwined on the floor of the camper van, mouths fused, hands roaming, pulling each other closer and closer until it seemed impossible that they were two separate bodies. There was no urgency to move, no need to start removing clothes, for hands to move lower. Not yet.

Seconds, minutes, hours, infinities passed by. All Jonas knew was the drumming of his blood in his ears, the fierce heat engulfing him. All he knew was her. Her touch, her taste, her mouth, the feel of her under his hands. When she pulled back it was as if she had been physically torn away from him, a painful wrench that left him cold. Empty.

She looked at him, eyes wide, dark with passion, her pupils dilated, mouth swollen. 'I think…' she began, her voice husky, barely audible.

Jonas readied himself. If she wanted to be the voice of common sense, so be it. He looked back at her silently. He might not argue, but he wasn't going to help her either.

'I think we should close the doors.'

Her words were so unexpected all he could do for a moment was gape. The van doors were still open to the night sky. The sea breeze floated in, bringing the taste of salt and the faint coconut-tinged smell of gorse.

Then the meaning of her words hit home. Anticipation filled the air, hot and heavy, making it hard to breathe as excitement coiled inside him.

'There's no one out there.'

They were in a secluded spot, parked at the very edge of the field. As private as you could be in a campsite full of tents and caravans. Not as private as they could have been if he'd planned for this.

'Even so...'

She smiled at him, slow and full of promise, and slowly, as if he were wading through treacle, he got to his feet and swung the sliding door firmly closed. The outside world was shut out. It was just the two of them in this small enclosed space. The air was heavy with expectation, with heat, with longing.

'Satisfied?' He raised an eyebrow and watched her flush.

'Not yet.' She was turning the tables on him. 'But I'm hoping to be.'

Passion jolted through him, intense and all-encompassing. In swift, sure steps he closed the space between them, pulling her in tight. 'Oh, you will be,' he promised as he lowered his mouth to hers once again. 'I can guarantee it.'

CHAPTER SEVEN

'Ooof!' When had breathing got so *hard*? Bending over to catch her breath, the tightness of a stitch pulling painfully at her side, Lawrie conceded that a ten-mile run might have been a mite ambitious.

Of course, she reassured herself, running outside was harder, what with all those hills and the wind against her, to say nothing of no nice speedometer to regulate her stride. Straightening up, one hand at her waist, Lawrie squinted out at the late-afternoon sun. On the other hand, she conceded, although her late, lamented treadmill came with TV screens and MP3 plug-ins it was missing the spectacular views of deep blue sea and rolling green and yellow gorse of her current circuit. It was definitely an improvement on the view of sweaty, Lycra-clad gym-goers that her old location had provided her with.

Taking a much needed long, cool gulp of water,

Lawrie continued at a trot, looping off the road and onto the clifftop path that led towards the village. If she continued along to the harbour she could reward herself with a refuelling stop at the Boat House before walking back up the hill home. No way was she going to try and run up that hill—not unless her fitness levels dramatically improved in the next half an hour.

Just keep going, she thought fiercely. *Concentrate on that latte...visualise it.* It was certainly one incentive.

And if Jonas just happened to be working at the Boat House today then that, just possibly, could be another incentive. The pain in her side was forgotten as the night before flashed through her mind, her lips curving in a smile as she remembered. Another night of heat, of long, slow caresses, hot, hard kisses, hands, tongues, lips. Bodies entwining.

Lawrie's pulse started to speed up as her heartbeat began racing in a way that had nothing to do with the exercise.

She upped the trot to a run, her legs pumping, her arms moving as she increased her pace. She wasn't going to think about it. She wasn't going to dwell on the delicious moment when day turned into evening. She wasn't going to remember the tingle of anticipation that ran through her as she sat on the terrace in the evening sun, an untouched book and an iced drink before her, pretending not to listen for the purr of his car. Pretending not to hope.

She was most certainly not going to recall the thrill that filled her entire body, the sweet jolt that shot through her from head to toe, when he finally appeared.

Time was moving so fast. She had less than a month left in Trengarth. So she wasn't going to question what was going on here. She was going to enjoy the moment. And what moments they were. She couldn't remember the last time she and Hugo had made love twice in a week, let alone in a night, whereas she and Jonas... Well...

Sure, she hadn't planned for this, and for once she was being the exact opposite of measured and sensible. But wasn't that the point? She had to make the most of this enforced time out. It would all get back to normal soon enough.

Starting with today. Her first interview.

It was all happening so fast. Just a few days

since the initial approach, the phone call, and now a face to face interview. In New York.

It was perfect. This would show Hugo and the partners. She could just imagine the gossip. *Lawrie Bennett? Out in New York, I believe. A most prestigious firm.* Anticipation shot through her. It was as if a load had been lifted. To be approached for such a role meant that her reputation was intact. It should be, but sudden departures were responsible for more scurrilous gossip in the legal world than any tabloid could imagine.

Lawrie slowed her pace as the cliff path began to wind down towards the harbour and the pretty stone cottages clustered beneath her. Which was Jonas's? He hadn't asked her over and she was certainly not going to invite herself, to admit she was curious.

Even if she was.

Was it the one overlooking the harbour, with the pretty roof garden situated in exactly the right place for the afternoon sun? The three-storeyed captain's house, imposing its grandeur on the smaller houses around? The long, low whitewashed cottage, its yard covered in tumbling roses?

What did it matter anyway?

Despite herself she slowed as she jogged along the harbour-front, looking into the windows, hoping for some clue. She didn't care, she told herself, but she still found herself craning her neck, peeking in, searching for a sign of him.

Beep!

A car horn made her jump. The follow-up wolf whistle which pierced the air brought her to a skidding halt.

Lawrie turned around, hands on hips, ready for battle, only to find her mouth drying out at the sight of Jonas Jones in that ridiculous low-slung sports car, top down. She coloured, looking around to make sure nobody had heard, before crossing the narrow road and leaning over the car. 'Shush. People will hear you,' she hissed.

He raised an eyebrow mockingly and Lawrie clenched her hands, controlling an irresistible urge to slap him. Or kiss him. Either would be inappropriate.

'Let them,' he replied nonchalantly, that annoying eyebrow still quirked.

She wanted to reach out and smooth it down,

caress the stubble on the strong jaw, run her fingers across the sensual lips. She clenched her hands harder. She wouldn't give him or the curious onlookers openly watching them the satisfaction.

Jonas leant closer, his breath warm and sweet on her cheek. 'They all think they know anyway.'

'Let them think. There's no need to confirm it.' She was painfully aware of people watching them—many openly. How many times had she seen neighbours, parents at the school gates, people in the local shop watch her mother in the same way as her latest relationship began to disintegrate? 'I hate gossip, and I really hate being the focus of it.'

'Just a boss having a chat with his festival-organiser—nothing to see…move it along,' he said, an unrepentant grin curving the kissable mouth.

She bit her lip. She was *not* going to kiss him in public, no matter how tempted she was. But how she wanted to.

Her eyes held his, hypnotised by the heat she saw in the blue depths. The street, the curious onlookers faded away for one long moment. She didn't know whether to be relieved or disappointed when he leant back, the grin replaced with a purposeful businesslike expression.

'I was on my way up to collect you—thought you might appreciate a lift to the airport. Yet here you are.' He ran his eyes appreciatively over her and she fought the urge to tug her running top down over her shorts. 'You're not really dressed for flying, though. And I don't mean to be offensive, but...'

Lawrie snorted. 'That will be a first,' she muttered.

'But I'm not sure eighties aerobics is really the right look for business class *or* an interview. You might want to get changed,' he continued, ignoring her interruption. 'I could give you a lift up—or, if you really want to finish your run, I can pick you up in ten minutes.'

'If you're in such a hurry I'd better take the lift,' Lawrie said, opening the door and sliding in, her pride refusing to admit to him that she'd had no intention of running up the hill. 'I was planning to drive myself, though. I do appreciate the offer, but can you spare the time?'

She sounded cool enough—shame about her

hair, pulled high into a sweaty bun, the Lycra shorts, the sheen of sweat on her arms and chest.

'Actually, it's on my way—that's why I'm offering. I'm heading over to Dorset to look at some potential sites. I'll be passing Plymouth so I might as well drop you off.'

'Oh.' He wasn't making the journey especially. Of course he wouldn't—why would he? Her sudden sharp jolt of disappointment was ridiculous. 'Well, it's very kind of you.'

There was a long silence. She sneaked a look over to see him pushing his hair out of his eyes, his face expressionless.

'It's nothing,' he said. 'As I said, I was passing the airport anyway.'

Neither of them spoke for the two minutes it took to drive back to the cottage, and as soon as the car pulled up in the driveway Lawrie was ready to leap out. The atmosphere was suddenly tense, expectant.

'I'll be five minutes,' she called as she hurried over the lawn and round to the back door. 'Make yourself at home.'

She fumbled with the key, breathing a sigh of relief as she finally pushed the door open, almost collapsing into the sanctuary of the kitchen, then heading straight to the bathroom to peel off her sweaty clothes and get into the welcome coolness of the shower.

The same peculiar feeling of disappointment gripped Lawrie as she lathered shampoo into her hair and over her body. What did it matter if he was dropping her off in passing or making the journey especially? Either way she ended up where she needed to be. Her trip to New York would be short—just a few days—but it meant time away from Cornwall, from the festival, from Jonas. Which was good, because their lives were already re-entangling, boundaries were being crossed. This interview was a much needed reminder that there was an end date looming and neither of them could or should forget that.

It had been a sweet kind of torture, watching her Lycra-clad bottom disappear around the corner. Jonas had to hold onto every ounce of his self-control to stay in the car and not follow her right into the shower, where he would be more than happy to help her take off those very tight and very distracting shorts.

He grabbed his coffee and took a long gulp.

This was temporary. They had always had an undeniable chemistry, even when nothing else between them had worked. And now they were both single, available, it was silly to deny themselves just because of a little bit of history.

Besides, they both knew what this was. No messy emotions, no need to prove anything. No need for words. It was the perfect summer fling.

It was all under control.

She'd said five minutes so he settled in for a half-hour wait, roof down, coffee in hand, paper folded to the business pages. But in less than fifteen minutes she reappeared, wheeling a small suitcase, laptop bag and handbag slung over her shoulder. She looked clean, fresh, so smooth he wanted nothing more than to drag her back inside and rumple her up a little—or a lot.

His hands clenched on the steering wheel as his pulse began to hammer, his blood heating up.

Damn that chemistry.

He dragged his eyes down from freshly washed, still-wet hair, combed back, to creamy skin—lots of it. Bare arms and shoulders, with just a hint of cleavage exposed by the halter-necked sundress, skirting her waist to fall mid-thigh.

He stifled a groan. He had a couple of hours' driving ahead of him and it was going to be hard to concentrate with so much skin nestled next to him.

'Is that suitable for flying? You'll need a cardigan,' he bit out, wrenching his gaze from the satisfied smile she gave him as she pulled a wispy wrap from the bag hung over her shoulder. 'Hurry up and get in. There's bound to be a lot of traffic.'

The powerful sports car purred along the narrow, winding lanes connecting Trengarth to the rest of the county. Lawrie leant back in the low leather seat, feeling the breeze ruffle her hair and watching the hedges and fields flash by. The blue glint of the sea was still visible in the distance, but soon the road would take them through the outskirts of Bodmin Moor, its rolling heathland and dramatic granite tors a startling contrast to her coastal home.

Home? She felt that pang again. Home was a dangerous concept.

'Lawrie?'

She jumped as Jonas repeated her name.

'Sorry, I was just daydreaming.'

'I know. I recognised that faraway look in your eyes,' he said wryly. 'Where were you? Round some boardroom table in New York?'

'Actually, I was thinking how beautiful it is round here.' That felt uncomfortably like a confession. 'No moors in New York.'

'No.'

Now it was his turn to stay silent, a brooding look on his face, as he navigated through open countryside and small villages until they met the main road. Suddenly the silence didn't feel quite so companionable, and after one uncomfortable minute that seemed to stretch out for at least five Lawrie began to search desperately for a topic of conversation.

It felt like a step backwards. Things had been so easy between them for the last few days—since the road trip, since that last night in the van. They had fallen into a pattern of colleagues by day, lovers by night—professional and focused at work, equally focused in the long, hot evenings.

Now she suddenly had no idea what to say.

'Will you be visiting your parents when you're in Dorset?'

Whatever had made her say that? Of all the topics in the world.

His face darkened. 'I doubt I'll have time.'

'You'll pass by their village, though, won't you? You should just pop in for a cup of tea.'

He didn't say anything, but she could see the tanned hands whiten as he gripped the steering wheel. She tried again, despite the inner voice telling her to back off, that it was none of her business. 'They must know the areas you're looking into. It might be interesting to hear their thoughts. Seems silly not to canvas local opinion, even if you don't take them into account.'

He was silent again. Lawrie sneaked a quick glance over, expecting to see anger, irritation in his expression. But he wasn't showing any emotion at all. She hated it—the way he could close himself off at will.

'I just think it's worth one more chance,' she said hesitantly. Why did she feel compelled to keep going with this? Because maybe this was one relationship she could fix for him? 'If they understood why you work the way you do—understood that you love Coombe End, that your changes are an evolution of their work, not a betrayal—maybe things would be better.'

He finally answered, his face forbidding. 'What makes you think I want things to be better?'

Lawrie opened her mouth, then shut it again. How could she tell him that where his parents were concerned she understood him better than he understood himself? That she knew how much he was shaped by his parents' indifference, how much he craved their respect?

'You're going to be in the area,' she said at last. 'Is popping in to see your parents such a big deal?'

He didn't answer and they continued the drive in silence. Lawrie stared unseeingly out at the trees and valleys as they flashed past, relieved when Jonas finally turned into the airport car park and pulled up at the dropping-off point.

'That's great—thank you.'

He didn't answer. Instead he got out of the car and walked round to the boot, retrieved her bag and laptop case as she smoothed her dress over her thighs and pushed herself out of the low seat.

It was hard to be dignified, getting out of a sports car.

'What time is your connection?'

She stared at him, wrenching her mind away from her thoughts to her surroundings. Back to her plans, her flight, her interview, her future. 'Oh, two hours after I get to Heathrow—which is plenty of time for Security, I hope.'

'Should be. Let me know if there are any changes with your flight back, otherwise I'll see you here.'

He was going to pick her up? Her heart lurched stupidly. 'You don't have to.'

'I know.'

'Okay, then.' She picked up her bags and smiled at him. 'Thanks, Jonas.'

'Good luck. They'd be mad not to offer you the job.'

'That's the hope.' She stepped forward and gave him a brief, light kiss, inhaling the fresh, seaside aroma of him as she did so, feeling an inexplicable tightening in her chest. 'Bye.'

He stood statue-still, not reacting to the kiss. 'Bye.'

She paused for a split second but she had no

idea what she was waiting for—why she had a sudden leaden feeling in the pit of her stomach. Taking a deep breath, she picked up the bags and, with a last smile in Jonas's direction, turned and walked away towards the sliding glass doors.

'Lawrie?'

She stopped, turned, unexpected and unwanted hope flaring up inside her.

'I'll make a deal with you. I'll go and visit my parents if you email your mother.'

The familiar panic welled up. 'I don't have her email address.'

'I can forward it to you.'

'Oh.' She searched for another excuse.

'Scared?' His voice was low, understanding, comforting.

'A little.' Not that she wanted to admit to fear—not to him. 'I don't know, Jonas. I feel safer with her not in my life.'

'I know.' His mouth twisted. 'It's just one step. It doesn't have to be more.'

Just one email. It sounded like such a small gesture and yet it felt so huge.

'One step,' she echoed. 'Okay.'

'Good. I'll see you here in four days.'

And he was gone.

* * *

Five hours later Lawrie was ensconced in a comfortable reclining seat, her laptop already plugged in on the table in front of her, her privacy screen blocking out the rest of the world.

Wriggling down into her seat, Lawrie squared her shoulders against the plump supporting cushions. She loved business class! The firm's willingness to pay for it boded well.

Ostensibly her ultra-comfortable journey should ensure she arrived in New York both well rested and prepared, but although her research on the firm was open on the laptop she had barely glanced at it.

Instead she had spent an hour composing an email to her mother. Lawrie reread the few short lines again and sighed. For goodness' sake, how hard could it be? She was aiming for polite, possibly even slightly conciliatory, but she had to admit the tone was off. The words sounded snooty, accusatory, *hurt*.

Exasperated, she deleted the lot and typed a few stiff sentences as if she were addressing a stranger.

She supposed she was. Would she even recognise her mother if she sat next to her? Her early teens were so long ago. Had it hurt her mother, leaving her only daughter in Trengarth? Never seeing her again?

Did she ever wonder if she had done the right thing? Regret her past?

She wondered how Jonas was doing with his parents—if his efforts were any more successful than her own.

She shook herself irritably. For goodness' sake! She was supposed to be preparing for her interview. This was it—her big chance.

So why did she feel so empty?

Lawrie slid a little further into the plush seat and looked out of the small window at the wispy white clouds drifting lazily past. What was wrong with her? Surely she hadn't let a blue eyed surfer derail her the way he had done twelve years ago?

Hot shame flushed through her body. She couldn't—wouldn't repeat the mistakes of her past. *Because let's face it*, she thought, *ambitious little Lawrie Bennett wanted many things*. She had planned her whole life through, and getting married the year she left school, before she'd received her A-level results, going to university as an eighteen-year-old bride had not been part of that plan.

Yet she had still said yes.

Lawrie pulled a piece of hair down and twizzled it around her finger. That moment—the utter joy that had suffused her whole being the second he'd asked her. Had she felt like that since? Not when she'd graduated with a first, not when she'd got hired at a top City firm.

And certainly not when Hugo had proposed.

She shook herself irritably, tucking the strand of hair back into her ponytail. Joy? 'For goodness' sake, grow up,' she muttered aloud. She was in business class, flying to be interviewed for the job of her dreams, and—what? It wasn't enough?

It was everything.

She had to remember that. *Everything.*

Jonas pulled over and typed the address into his phone, but he knew long before the icon loaded that he was in the right place. Looking around the tree-lined lane, he saw a row of identikit 1930s detached houses, all painted a uniform white, every garden perfectly manicured, every drive guarded by large iron gates, every car a sleek saloon. There wasn't a plastic slide or football goal to be seen.

The quiet, still road was crying out for bikes to be pedalled along it, the wide pavements for chalk and hopscotch. But there was no one to be seen.

Jonas sighed. What was he doing here? How many times could a guy set himself up for disappointment? He wouldn't be welcome. Even if his parents liked surprises his unheralded appearance wasn't going to bring them any joy.

But he had made a deal. And he might not know much about Lawrie Bennett any more, but he did know that there was something lost at the heart of her.

That desperate need to fit in, to be in control. To follow the plan...

He'd tried to fill that void once. Maybe someone in New York could, if she could just let go of her fears. And if he could do that much for his ex-wife—well, maybe their marriage wouldn't have been such a disaster after all.

A sharp pain twisted inside him at the thought of her with someone else but he ignored it. One of them deserved to be happy; one of them should be. And himself? Well… He smiled wryly. There were moments. Moments when a deal went well, when a chord was played right, when he looked around at a café full of content customers, when a wave was perfect.

Those moments were gold. He didn't ask for more. He wasn't sure he was capable of more.

Sighing, Jonas looked down at the icon on his phone, busily flashing away, signalling a road just to the left. He was pretty sure the next few moments were going to be anything but gold. But he'd promised.

And he always kept his word.

Why did his parents favour cups that were so damn small? And chairs that were so damn uncomfortable? And wallpaper that was so very, very busy? And, really, would it hurt them to smile?

The silence stretched on, neither side willing to break it. Side? That, thought Jonas, was a very apt word. Somehow—so long ago he had no idea when or why—they had become entrenched on opposite sides of a chasm so huge Jonas didn't think there was any way across it at all.

'So...' he said slowly. Speaking first felt like giving in, but after all he *had* intruded on them. 'I was just passing...'

'Where from?'

Did he just imagine that his mother sounded suspicious? Although, to be fair, he hadn't been 'just passing' in four years—not since the day he had told them that he had bought their beloved hotel.

'I was dropping Lawrie off at the airport.'

'Lawrie? You're back together?'

Now *that* emotion he could identify. It was hope. Even his father had looked up from his teacup, sudden interest in his face. Lawrie was the only thing he'd ever done that they'd approved of—and they hadn't been at all surprised when she'd left him.

'She's working for me this summer. Just a temporary thing before she moves to New York. And, no, we're not back together.' It wasn't a lie. Whatever was going on, they weren't back together.

'Oh.'

The disappointment in his mother's voice was

as clear as it was expected. Jonas looked around, desperate for something to catch his eye—another conversation-starter. A spectacularly hideous vase, some anaemic watercolours… But something was lacking—had always been lacking. And it wasn't a simple matter of wildly differing tastes.

'Why don't you have any photos?' he asked abruptly.

The room was completely devoid of anything personal. Other people's parents displayed their family pictures as proudly as trophies: bald, red-faced babies, gap-toothed schoolchildren, self-conscious teens in unflattering uniforms.

The silence that filled the room was suddenly different, charged with an emotion that Jonas couldn't identify.

His mother flushed, opened her mouth and shut it again.

'Dad?'

Jonas stared at his father, who was desperately trying to avoid his eye, looking into the depths of the ridiculously tiny teacup as if it held the answer to the secret of life itself.

'Dad,' he repeated.

The anger he had repressed for so long—the anger he'd told himself he didn't feel, the anger that was now boiling inside him—was threatening to erupt. He swallowed it back, tried to sound calm, not to let them know that he felt anything.

'I know I'm not the son you wanted, but—really? Not even one photo?'

'Leave it, Jonas,' his father said loudly, putting his cup down so decidedly it was a miracle the thin china didn't break in two.

'Why?' he persisted.

He would not leave it. For so many years he had endured their disapproval and their silence, their refusal to engage with him. He'd listened to their instructions, to their plans for his life—and then he'd gone ahead and done what he wanted anyway. But suddenly he couldn't leave it—didn't want to walk away.

He wanted answers.

'I appreciate that I don't live my life the way you want me to, that I didn't make the most of the opportunities you gave me, and I admit that failing my exams at sixteen wasn't the smartest move.'

He tried a smile but got nothing back. His father was still trembling with some repressed emotion; his mother was pale, still as stone.

'But,' he carried on, determined that *this* time they would hear him, *this* time he would have his say, 'I have an MBA, I have a successful business, I own a house, I'm a good boss, I give to charity.' Despite himself, despite his best intentions, his voice cracked. 'I just don't know why I have never been good enough for you.'

There. It was said.

The silence rippled round the room.

His mother got to her feet, so pale her carefully applied make-up stood out stark against her skin. 'I can't do this, Jonas,' she said.

He stared at her in astonishment. Were those tears in her eyes?

'I'm sorry, I just can't.' She laid one, shaky hand on his shoulder for an infinitesimal second and then was gone, rushing out of the room.

What the hell...? He'd expected indifference, or anger, or some lecture about what a waste of space he had always been, but this tension strung as tight as a quivering bow was unexpected. It was terrifying. Whatever was going on here was bigger than the fall-out of some adolescent re-bellion.

Jonas glared at his father, torn between utter confusion and sudden fear. 'Dad? What *is* going on? I think I deserve the truth, don't you?'

CHAPTER EIGHT

IT WAS HORRENDOUSLY hot, and the airport was overcrowded as families, couples, grandparents waited anxiously, pressing close to the gate, necks craning for the first glimpse of a loved one.

Some had even brought signs—handwritten, decorated. Jonas looked over at the young man barely out of his teens, standing at the very end, as close as he could get to the gate without crossing the yellow line. He had love hearts all over his sign. The poor sap.

He even had flowers, Jonas noted. A bouquet so big it almost obscured the sign.

Whereas it was all Jonas had been able to do to turn up at all. He was still processing the afternoon he had spent with his parents. He wasn't sure he could share it with anyone, and Lawrie was bound to ask.

After all they had a deal.

'Hey.'

He hadn't even seen her come through the gate. 'Hey, yourself. Good trip?'

She beamed. 'The best. They're a really exciting firm, with some great projects, so fingers crossed they liked me.'

'I bet they loved you.' He took her bag from her and led the way out of the airport to the short-stay car park. Suddenly, despite everything, the day seemed brighter, the clouds drifting away. It was too nice to be shut away in an office—even his office.

'Are you exhausted?' he asked.

Lawrie shook her head. 'I might have had a red-eye flight, but I was spoiled enough to spend it tucked up in business class. I feel fresh as a daisy! I swear those seats are comfier than my bed.'

'I was thinking a picnic,' he said. 'There's a nice farmshop about twenty minutes away where we could grab some supplies. Unless you want to get back?'

Lawrie looked down at herself and pulled a face, although Jonas thought she looked immaculate, in dark skinny jeans that clung to her legs in a way he definitely approved of.

'I need a shower at some point in the next few hours,' she said. 'No matter how air-conditioned the airport and plane are, I still land feeling completely grubby. But fresh air sounds good, and I guess I could eat. My business class freshly cooked breakfast seems a long time ago now.'

'Nice subtle reminder of your exalted status.' Jonas nodded approvingly. 'You'll need to up the stakes when you get to New York, though, I believe lawyers on the Upper East Side only travel by private jet.'

'Ha-ha.' Lawrie stuck her tongue out at him as they reached the car and he opened the door for her before stowing her cases in the boot.

'Your post is on your seat,' he called over. 'I knew you would want to look through it before you relaxed properly.'

'Thanks,' she called back.

Closing the door, he saw she was already engrossed, flipping through the pile and sorting the mail into order. She was up to date with her emails too, he knew. Lawrie wouldn't allow a little thing like the Atlantic Ocean to stand between her and her work.

A good reason to make sure she had the afternoon off. And it would probably do him good too. He'd barely left his desk these last two days. Sometimes hard work was the only way to cope.

He slid into his seat and looked over at her. She was staring at an envelope, her cheeks pale. He recognised it: a thick, expensive cream envelope with the name of her old firm stamped on the back. It was probably her P45 or something.

It didn't explain the pallor in her cheeks, though.

'Everything okay?' He turned the key and felt the engine purr into life.

She didn't answer.

'Law?'

She looked across, a dazed expression on her face. 'Hmm? Yes, I'm fine.'

But she didn't sound convincing.

'Are you going to open that?' He nodded towards the envelope. She was turning it over and over, as if she could read the contents through touch alone.

'Yes, of course. It's probably some HR stuff.'

But she looked anxious as she tore the envelope open, pulling out a handwritten letter with another slip of paper clipped to the outside. It looked like a cheque.

'What on earth…?'

'Redundancy?' he suggested.

She shook her head. 'That will get paid with my last month's salary, and not until my notice is completely served,' she said, unfolding the letter and slipping the cheque out. Her eyes widened. 'My goodness—how many noughts?' Then, her voice seemed strangled with what sounded suspiciously like tears. 'It's from Hugo.'

The ex.

Jealousy, ugly and hot, seared through him. What was he doing writing to her? Sending her cheques?

Grimly he set his eyes on the road ahead, concentrating on the exit from the airport, trying to give Lawrie the space she needed as she fought for control.

'It's for my share of the house,' she said after a while, her voice a little croaky. 'He didn't have to. I mean, yes, I contributed to the bills, of course—paid for decorating and stuff. But it was his house. Legally I'm not entitled to anything. My name wasn't on the mortgage.'

Was she regretting leaving him? A man who made such generous gestures? Thoughtful? 'Will you accept?'

There was a pause.

'Yes,' she said finally. 'My pride tells me to shred it and return it to him, but he's right. If I hadn't moved in with him I'd have bought my own place, made money on that. This cheque is enough for a reasonable deposit so I can buy in New York, or wherever I end up. I'd be a fool to turn it down. And I guess morally I do deserve it.'

She was silent again as she read the rest of the letter, all her attention on the closely written lines until an exclamation burst out, her voice high with shock 'He's getting married! In September. His fiancée is pregnant so they're rushing it through.'

Indignation replaced the jealousy.

'He has a *fiancée*? A *pregnant* fiancée? How on earth did he manage that? You've only been apart a couple of weeks! Unless he was cheating on you?'

The colour in her cheeks gave him the answer.

Jonas whistled softly. 'What a bastard!'

Lawrie didn't answer for a bit, turning the letter over to read it again. 'No. He isn't—not really.'

It was odd, listening to her defend another man. A man she had lived with.

'Okay, that's not entirely true. He behaved horribly, but I think it was my fault—at least partly.' She whispered the last part, tears choking her voice again.

Jonas's first instinct was to pull over, to pull her into his arms and comfort her. But one look at her rigid face as she fought for control dissuaded him. She was so private, so secretive, he instinctively knew she'd clam up if he offered sympathy.

He kept his voice impersonal. 'Your fault how? Because you left?'

'Because I didn't love him. Not in the way he deserved to be loved. I see that now.' She looked away, out of the window, and when she spoke again her voice was level. Composed. 'I wasn't entirely honest with you. It was just too humiliating. I didn't leave Hugo. I didn't change the plan. It was changed for me the day I found him with someone else. If it had been up to me I'd still be there, working towards making partner, putting off planning my wedding, engaged to someone I couldn't admit I didn't love.'

'He didn't deserve you.' Jonas knew that absolutely. If he had he would have been faithful.

She shook her head. 'He really did love me once. And I wanted to love him, I thought I did, but…' She faltered. 'Ouch—honesty hurts, doesn't it? Truth is, I think it was the lifestyle I wanted—the package. He should have someone who doesn't care about the package, who wants him because he is kind and decent.' She sniffed. A slight sound that almost broke his heart. 'I hope he's found that.'

'That's big of you. Really.'

When Lawrie had left him the last thing he'd wished for was her happiness. It shamed him to remember how bitter he had been.

'There was a point when I could happily have castrated him with a spoon,' she admitted. 'And strangled *her* with her own leopard print thong.'

Jonas's eyebrows rose at the extraordinary visual and he tried his best to control a smirk. A watery giggle next to him confirmed his failure.

'But I was more unhappy about having to leave the firm than about the infidelity. I think, if he'd offered I would have allowed him to grovel and pretend I hadn't seen anything. Wow, I'm pitiful.'

'That *is* a little sad,' he agreed. 'But why did you have to be the one to go?'

'Because his grandfather founded the firm. Oh, my payoff will be good, my reference glowing— as it should be!—but it was made clear that they would prefer me to pack up, get out and keep my mouth shut. And I was too embarrassed to fight.' She sighed. 'So there you are—the big, ugly truth. The real reason I turned up at the Boat House alone on my thirtieth. Do you hate me?'

'I think you're amazing,' Jonas said.

He honestly did. This woman was strong—a survivor.

'And I'm glad you found your way home to Trengarth. Even if it's just for the summer.' He reached over and put his hand on her knee. 'I'm glad I've had this opportunity to know you again. And,' he added with a teasing smile, 'you're a great project manager!'

'So...' Lawrie lay back on the picnic blanket, looking up at the sky. 'I did it. Are you proud?'

'Did what?'

Jonas knew exactly what she was talking about. He still didn't know what he was going to say— if he could be honest.

He opted for diversionary tactics. 'Ate your own body weight? Because I have to say that was a pretty impressive amount of food.'

'I blame the sea air,' Lawrie said thoughtfully. 'I never ate like this in London. It's a good thing I'm off soon—there isn't enough exercise in the world… But, no, that's not what I meant. I emailed my mother. Proud?'

'Mmm,' he said noncommittally. Aware of her sudden keen scrutiny, Jonas tried for more enthusiasm. 'That's great. Did she reply?'

It was Lawrie's turn to sound less than enthusiastic. 'Oh, yes—a great long stream of consciousness that was all about her.' She pulled a face. 'Not one question about me or what I'm doing.'

Jonas propped himself up on an elbow and looked down at her. 'I'm sorry.'

'Don't be.' Lawrie sat up, wrapping her arms around her knees and staring out to sea. 'Of course she *is* monumentally self-centred—I knew that. What kind of woman ditches her teenage daughter to go trekking? Doesn't come to her own mother's funeral? Truth is, I've spent my whole life hating her and at the same time wanting her to put me first, you know? But reading that email I just felt sorry for her. Which is an improvement, I guess. And I know she isn't capable of more. I just have to accept that.'

She turned to him, her face alight with interest. 'So…?'

'So?'

Here it was. And he still didn't know what to say.

'Did you go?'

The sand suddenly felt lumpy, hard beneath his elbow, and Jonas lay down. It was his turn to look up at the clear blue sky, the wisps of cloud lazily bobbing overhead. The weight of his newly acquired burden pressed down on him. Maybe sharing would help.

If anything could.

And Lawrie would be going soon. She wouldn't be there to constantly remind him, asking him how he felt, looking at him with sympathy or pity. And if she recoiled from him in disgust—well, maybe he deserved it.

'Yes,' he said slowly. 'I went.'

'And...?'

She seemed to sense the turmoil in him, was looking down at him in concern.

'Jonas, what is it? What did they say?'

He took a deep breath. 'I asked them why they had no photos of me—not one anywhere.' The words were almost dragged out of him, yet the very act of saying them relieved some of the almost unbearable load his father had bequeathed to him.

Lawrie was utterly still, her concentration all fixed on him. 'And...?'

'At first? Nothing. Then finally my father admitted they couldn't bear to—couldn't bear to have pictures of their only son. It was too painful a reminder.' He exhaled noisily. 'My presence, my *existence*, is too painful a reminder.'

He turned his head to look at her, to see her reaction as he finally said the words.

'There were two of us, Law. I had a twin—a sister. But we were early...too early. I was a lot bigger than her, so when we were born I had a better chance. She was too small.' He paused, remembering the utter look of desolation, of loss, on his father's face as he'd stumbled through the family secret.

'The doctors said if I hadn't taken up so much of the blood supply things could have been different—they might have saved us both. But as it was I killed her, Law. I killed my twin sister.'

For an agonisingly long time Lawrie didn't say anything. Was she horrified at him? By him? By what he had done? Because *he* was. This explained everything, and suddenly he couldn't blame his parents at all.

She was bolt upright, one hand covering her mouth, tears swimming in her eyes. One was falling and rolling unheeded down her cheek. With a muffled sob she turned to him, her arms reaching out, enfolding him, pulling him close, pulling him in.

'You poor boy,' she whispered, her tears soaking into his hair. 'It wasn't your fault—you hear me? Don't let *anyone* put this horrible thing onto you. It wasn't your fault.'

Jonas knew he should pull away, that the temptation to sink into her and never let go was too strong right now—that letting her go might be the hardest thing he had ever had to do. But the relief of another person's touch, another person's warmth, was too much, too intoxicating for a long, blissful moment, and he bathed in her warmth, in her understanding, before pulling back, reaching for her hand, lacing her fingers into his.

'If I had been a different kind of boy it might all have been easier,' he said after a while, caressing the soft smoothness of her hand. 'If I had been more like them…quieter…maybe they could have accepted me. But I was so boisterous, so energetic—always wanting to be different. I was always showing them how strong I was, how healthy. A constant reminder that if I had been a little *less* strong then she might have made it too.'

'No.'

The strength in her voice surprised him, her conviction ringing true.

'No. You mustn't ever think that. What happened was horrible—*horrible*. Your poor parents…I can't even imagine…' She shuddered. 'But it was no one's fault. Especially not yours.' She shook her head. 'And although I feel desperately sorry for your parents I could also shake them. Pushing you away, rather than thanking

God every moment that they were blessed with one healthy, amazing boy? That's their tragedy. And they have to live with it. But you…' Her fingers tightened on his. 'You let this go.'

They sat, hands entwined, staring out to sea, neither of them speaking, and gradually, slowly, Jonas felt some of the darkness lift. He would always have to carry this knowledge, this loss, with him, but Lawrie was right. He didn't have to let it define him—even if his parents had allowed it to define their lives, their relationship with him.

There was nothing he could do about that. His card had been marked from the moment of his birth. He just had to live with that and move on— properly this time.

'At least…' he said slowly. 'At least I know it wasn't me—some terrible defect in me. I used to wonder, you know…wonder why they couldn't love me…why I was so damn unlovable.'

'Lots of people love you.' Lawrie leant in close, her hair soft on his cheek. 'Gran loved you—she adored you. When I left—when we split up—she told me I was a fool, that there was no finer man out there. Who knows? Maybe she was right.'

'She was definitely right,' he said, and was rewarded with a low laugh. 'Thank you,' he said. 'For listening.'

She turned to him, eyes serious. 'You know, I thought coming back here was going to be the most humiliating experience—facing you again, no job, no Hugo.' She shook her head. 'And it was pretty awful at first, but in a way I'm glad. That we got the chance to reconnect. To be friends again.'

'Is that what the kids call it nowadays?'

She smiled, moving her hand up to push the hair from his eyes in an old, intimate gesture. 'I believe the phrase says "with benefits".'

He stared deep into her eyes, watched her pupils darken, grow, heard her breath quicken. His hand caressed hers, moving down to circle the delicate skin at her wrist. Right now all he wanted, needed, was to lose himself in this person who believed in him, who had once needed him.

'I, for one,' he said, 'am a great fan of benefits. I think they should be explored in much greater detail.'

Her pulse leapt at his touch. 'How great?'

'Let's go home,' he said. 'And I'll show you.'

CHAPTER NINE

DAMN, SHE WAS daydreaming again.

It was this office. Too much space, too many large windows with far too beautiful views. It just wasn't conducive to concentration. She'd choose her old windowless, airless, tiny internal office over this spacious luxury any day. At least she'd never been distracted there.

And it *was* the view, the sun, the come-hitherness of the summer's day that was the problem. It was not—most certainly *not*—the last few days.

Lawrie gazed unseeingly at the complicated document in front of her, detailing band schedules, riders, accommodation, entourage lists, her mind churning.

After the initial awful shock, the sudden grief and guilt, Jonas had seemed freed, unburdened. And hellbent on getting as much benefit out of their newfound friendship as he possibly could.

And she was matching him every step of the way.

She told herself it was because she was worried about him, because he seemed to be coping too well, because she could still see the hurt behind the playboy smile, but the selfish truth was that the benefits were working both ways.

Working really well.

It was no good. For once work was letting her down. Maybe she needed to take a break.

Sitting up, she grabbed her phone and flicked to her personal emails—belated birthday greetings from friends who didn't even know she'd left London, the usual deluge of sales emails offering her shoes, spa days, holidays, clothes. None of it mattered. Not any more.

'That's rather a scary grimace. Planning some street theatre?'

She looked up with a start. 'Some warning would be nice. You shouldn't sneak in like that.' It was the shock that had made her heart leap—not the sight of Jonas, immaculate in tennis whites, legs bronzed and muscular, hair damp with exertion pushed back off his forehead.

After all, *any* passable man looked good in tennis clothes.

Still, despite herself, she let her gaze travel from the dark blond tip of his head down over broad shoulders to his chest, clearly outlined through the fine white material, down past the shorts that clung to his narrow hips far too comfortably for her peace of mind and down those rather magnificent legs.

Lawrie swallowed, desperate to moisten her suddenly dry mouth as a jolt of desire pulsed through her, as a sweet, persistent ache settled in the pit of her stomach.

'You look like you've been busy.'

'Got to make sure all the facilities are in perfect working order.' He grinned at her boyishly. 'It's a hard job, but someone has to do it.'

Sauntering across the room, Jonas perched next to her on the edge of her desk.

Lawrie swallowed, the spreadsheet, her emails all forgotten. There was so *much* of him, and it was all so close. So much toned, tanned flesh, perfectly set off by the white fabric. Too much of the overwhelmingly male scent evoking grass, sun and sea. She licked her lips nervously, unsure whether she wanted to push the self-assured interloper off the desk or push him back and straddle him.

'And are they? In working order?'

Goodness, why did everything sound like a *double entendre*?

'Of course.' He smiled at her, slow and sweet. 'Want to find out?'

'No, I haven't played in years.' And she looked away from his knowing grin, feeling the heat spreading downwards, pooling in the pit of her belly. She tried again. 'I don't really have time to play. I watch a little, though. The firm had a corporate box at Wimbledon.'

He pulled a face. 'Wining and dining clients, hospitality boxes—it's all right for some, I suppose. It's not the real deal, though, is it?'

'It's different,' she said, ruthlessly pushing aside memories of being trapped in conversation with CEOs who knew nothing and cared less about the top-quality tennis being played out before them, who were there solely because it showed that they were *somebody*.

'But not better?' He was still sitting by her, dis-concertingly close, one trainer-clad foot swing-ing. 'Although I hear the queuing facilities are much better now, and people have proper tents and loos and everything.' He put on a quavery voice. 'People today don't know they're born. In my day a couple of fold-up chairs and a sleeping bag did us.'

'Men's quarter-finals day,' she remembered. The sound of the racket hitting the ball, the smell of grass mingling with traffic fumes and sun cream, the taste of sweet, succulent strawberries, rich cream, and Pimm's fizzing on her tongue. 'Seems so long ago. We saw Agassi!'

He laughed. 'You can keep your Seychelles and your Maldives. A dusty pavement and top-quality tennis is the perfect honeymoon destination in my book. You wanted me to buy you an Agassi T-shirt!'

She laughed with him, couldn't help it. 'Well, I *was* eighteen,' she defended herself. 'Have you been since?'

He shook his head. 'June and July are such busy times for me. Pete, our pro, usually goes—takes some of the local kids he coaches—but I haven't joined them yet. One day.'

She nodded her agreement and tried to think of something else to say. Hard to think with him so close, so casual, so overpowering, so very male. Her mouth was dry, her mind suddenly empty. *Say something, damn it,* she thought. She opened her mouth but no sound came out.

'I was going to go for a swim,' Jonas said, seemingly unaware of her awkwardness.

Didn't he feel the uncomfortable silence? The weight of their past happiness?

'Fancy it?'

'Oh, I…well…' She fumbled desperately for the right words. If she was finding Jonas hard to cope with when he was semi-respectably clad in tennis whites then how would she manage with him wearing nothing but swim shorts? 'I haven't brought anything suitable to swim in,' she finished.

'Good thing we have a shop,' he said, and his eyes took on a disconcerting gleam. 'Or you could just wear nothing at all…'

For a long second Lawrie couldn't breathe. All she could do was stare at him, hypnotised by the heat in his eyes, the way the blue deepened until she was drowning in their azure depths. The ache in her stomach intensified, moved even lower, and for one hot, blazing moment all she was aware of was him.

Zzzzzzz.

Lawrie jumped. The buzz of her phone as it signalled the arrival of a text message broke the spell. Blinking her way slowly into reality, she realised in one mortifying moment that she was leaning forward, moving closer to him. With an effort she wrenched her gaze away, leaning back and looking intently at her computer as if all the answers were to be found there.

She summoned up a light, amused tone. 'I thought this was a respectable family hotel?'

Jonas still looked ridiculously at ease, seemingly unaware of her struggle to stay focused. 'It is—and I have something a bit more refreshing in mind than a pool full of overtired toddlers and harassed parents. Ready?'

Sensible Lawrie, clipboard-touting, plan-making Lawrie, knew it was a bad idea. She glanced at the spreadsheets still open on her desk. The safe, easy option. The right option.

But not the only option.

Just a couple of weeks left. A short while to be someone else. Someone less measured, less careful, less controlled. Someone free.

And then she would go to New York, Sydney, Toronto—wherever—and this summer would be a dream, a memory.

Someone else.

A smile curved her lips. She took a deep breath, kicked the chair back, away from the desk, and swivelled it towards Jonas, still sitting there on the desk, onc bare leg idly swinging, watching her with an impenetrable gaze.

'Let's go,' she said.

Lawrie felt like a schoolgirl playing hooky as Jonas led her across a field at the back of the hotel garden towards the path that led down to the cove bordering the hotel property. It wasn't a private beach, but as there was no public right of way to it, it was used solely by hotel guests and anyone with access to a boat.

'Feels good doesn't it?'

'What does?'

'Being outside when you should be at work.'

'But you're my boss,' she pointed out as they slowed to a jog. 'And as I'm not being paid I'm not sure this technically counts as skiving.'

He shook his head, a mischievous smile playing around the sensual lips. 'Admit it—you still feel half guilty, though, I bet this is the first time you've ever bunked off work.'

She didn't answer, increasing her pace so that she sprinted past him, enjoying the sun on her face, the slight breeze ruffling her hair, the unusually giddy feeling of being free. Jonas gave a startled shout as she raced ahead, before also breaking into a fast run, catching her up with long-legged strides, elbowing his way past her to reach the stile first.

'Aren't you glad I made you get changed?' he asked, glancing down at her shorts and vest top appreciably. 'Those power heels of yours wouldn't have lasted five minutes.'

She pulled a face before darting round him and jumping over the stile onto the path that wound round the cliff, sniffing appreciatively. Gorse—how she loved it.

Jonas leant against the stile post, watching her. 'You look like a Labrador off after a scent.'

'It just smells so good,' she explained, knowing how idiotic she sounded.

It was funny… She'd read that smell was the best sense to evoke memories but she had never really noticed it personally before. Yet ever since she had returned to Cornwall she'd found herself reliving, remembering, her memories triggered by the very air about her. A primal creature after all, despite her veneer of city sophistication.

Jonas stepped up beside her and his hand brushed against hers. Such a small touch to provoke such intense memories. Long, lean, capable fingers entwined round hers. She felt the coolness of his palm, the slight roughness of his skin. She was preternaturally aware of every tiny square millimetre where their flesh touched, of little trickles of desire rippling up her arm. Her breasts suddenly felt full, heavy, aching, and an almost painful pressure behind her ribs echoed the intensified beating of her heart. Did he know? Was he aware of the effect his slightest touch had on her?

She didn't speak. Didn't look down at their hands. Didn't acknowledge him in any way. But she didn't pull away either.

Lost in a haze of feeling, Lawrie was unaware of where they were walking, knowing only the heady joy of touch, smell, sensation until they reached the top of the cliff.

'Where are we?' she asked looking about her in some confusion. 'This isn't the hotel beach.'

'Nope, this is the next cove along,' he explained. 'The hotel beach will be full of guests and their families, and mini-tot surf schools, sandcastle-building. All perfectly lovely, but a little more crowded than I had in mind.'

He looked back and flashed her a grin of such pure, seductive wickedness that her knees weakened and she nearly stumbled, steadying herself against the sparsely covered cliff-face with one trembling hand.

He means swimming, she told herself. *Get a grip.*

'Careful,' he called back as she picked her way down the dirt track. 'There're lots of little stones—it's easy to slip.'

'I do know how to walk down a cliff path,' she told him, but she slowed down a little, dragging her mind away from his earlier comments and her own overheated imaginings until she reached the bottom and looked about her.

It was a tiny little cove—a perfect little semi-circle of fine sand leading down to lapping waves, hidden from the rest of existence by the tall cliffs whose arms reached out into the sea on either side. A few rocks clustered at the foot of the cliff.

Jonas was standing by a large flat one and had laid the small rucksack he was carrying on top, was already shaking out the tartan blanket and laying out a couple of towels.

'It's beautiful,' Lawrie said, looking around in delight. 'I can't believe I've never been here before.'

'You can't access it from Trengarth,' Jonas said. 'With the hotel so close nobody ever comes here. Which is why I like it.'

Having taken care of the contents of the rucksack he was kicking off his trainers, pulling his T-shirt over his head. She stared, fascinated, at the still slim but perfectly toned chest, at the smattering of golden hair over his well-formed pecs turning into a fascinating line running down his taut stomach and disappearing into the top of his swim shorts.

Lawrie swallowed, an insistent pulse of desire throbbing through her entire body.

'Come on,' he teased her, moving from foot to foot.

Reluctantly she tore her eyes from his torso and looked out at the sea. Yes, it was calm, blue, inviting, and it was August, but even so...

He followed her gaze and sighed. 'Wimp,' he said. 'Honestly, when we were kids we swam in just our costumes Easter to October—now it's wetsuits all year round. Does no one like the feel of water on their skin any more?'

'You always liked your wetsuit well enough,' she retorted. But, stung by his words, she reluctantly pulled off her vest top, glad that she had bought a modest one-piece from the hotel shop and not the skimpy bikini he had picked out for her.

'I like my wetsuit for surfing, when I'm in the water for hours at a time, not for a good swim. The cold's half the fun.' He eyed her as she slipped the shorts off, an appreciative glint in his eye. 'That's not the itsy-bitsy polka-dot bikini I picked out, but it's rather nice.'

She looked down at herself. The fifties-style

swimsuit suited her, she thought. The nipped in waist added curves to her leanness; the halter-style neckline lifted her breasts. He was still looking at her, his eyes lingering on the hint of cleavage, the exposed tops of her breasts. Feeling suddenly, unaccountably shy she took a step back, towards the sea.

'Last one in is a rotten egg,' Lawrie said, and took off, running towards the sea.

Jonas stood still for one disbelieving second before he took off after her, running up behind her, swinging her into his arms and running them both headlong into the sea until he was waist-high when, despite her laughing entreaties, he dropped her straight into the cold, clear water.

It was freezing. Like little shards of ice on her overheated skin. She sank beneath the surface, spluttering with outrage, with laughter, with cold. Her feet found the sandy bottom and she steadied herself and stood up, revenge on her mind.

Jonas had already anticipated her mood and was swimming away from her, widthways across the bay, reaching out with sure, sharp strokes. She stood for a minute, pushing her wet hair away from her face, blinking the water out of her eyes and watching him—sleek, strong, completely at home in the marine environment he loved. He turned, floating onto his back, and gave her a little ironic wave.

Right. She set out across the water. Goodness, it was hard work swimming against the waves; a flat gym pool was no substitute for the sea. Forgetting Jonas for a second, she stopped swimming, treading water and allowing the waves to bob her up and down, closing her eyes and enjoying the sensation of the hot sun contrasting with the cold sea, the sound of the waves, the seagulls overhead—until a splash of sea water on her face brought her back to the present with a startled cry.

'You…' she threatened scooping up some water and flinging it at him.

Laughing, he dodged out of the way. Lawrie pursued him, pushing more and more water at him, until with a triumphant yell she doused him, moving in, holding him back whilst she thoroughly dunked him, enjoying the feeling of power, the play of muscles in his shoulders as she held him down, enjoying the way their bodies entwined as they play-fought. The hardness of him, the strength… She shivered.

He stopped fighting her, suddenly still, waist-deep in the sea. Her hands stilled on his shoulders as he straightened, and her wet body was close to his as one of his arms came to rest loosely round her waist. The other was at the nape of her neck until he drew a slow, tantalising line down her bare spine, his hand coming to rest on the small of her back, his long, oh, so capable fingers drawing a slow circle. Every sense she had seemed to be centred in that small area of sensitised skin.

'Jonas?'

It was such a small sound—a question, an entreaty? She couldn't have said. She just knew that she needed something—something more, something only this man could give her. She moved in closer, leg against leg, her aching breasts pressed against the tautness of his chest, her face raised pleadingly to his. This was why they had come here, wasn't it? For this…for the sheer sweetness of the moment as he finally lowered his mouth to hers.

Light kisses, delicate kisses, lips against lips,

murmured endearments and still such restraint. One of his hands was still caressing the small of her back, the other was lightly on her waist as she held onto his shoulders, pressing herself closer against him, trying to get more of him, to deepen the kiss, to lose control.

Just for a while. Just for now, for this moment.

He picked her up again, swinging her up as if she weighed no more than a child, his arms tight around her. Without saying a word he strode towards the shore.

Lawrie felt a dreamlike calm mixed with an almost unbearable anticipation as she wound her arms around his neck and snuggled in, pressing small butterfly kisses onto the side of his neck. Her tongue flicked out, tasting the salt, and he gave a groan. Emboldened, she carried on exploring the wet, golden flesh, following drops of water with her lips, enjoying the effect she was clearly having on him.

He reached the picnic blanket and knelt down, placing her carefully onto it. She lay there waiting, welcoming, wanting, rolling towards him as he lay beside.

She needed this…she *deserved* this.

'Lawrie?'

His eyes were dark with desire, and the fire she saw in them elicited a primal response in her. The ache pulsating between her thighs was insistent, strong, powerful. She didn't answer. Words were beyond her. She was all instinct, all desire. She rose to her knees and leant over, pressing her mouth to his, her arms on either side of him supporting her weight.

With a groan he grabbed onto her, rolling her on top of him, deepening the kiss as his hands finally moved away from her waist, roaming over her body, touching, caressing, lighting sparks everywhere they travelled. She was aware of nothing but him, the planes of his body, the sensations his oh, so skilled fingers were inducing in her, his kiss, the taste of him, the feel of his lips, his tongue.

Sun, sea, salt, sensation overwhelmed her, whisking Lawrie away to some faraway place where all that existed was this. All that existed was them, just as it had used to be. She closed her eyes, allowing his touch, his mouth, his body to take her away, to soar over the cliffs and spiral up into the sky.

* * *

Jonas lay stretched out on the blanket, Lawrie curved into his side, one arm flung lightly across his chest. She was dozing, almost asleep but not quite, her eyes closed, her breathing even. Despite the lateness of the hour the air was still warm, sticky. He felt...*content*. That was the nearest word for the relaxed laziness of his body and mind.

For once Jonas didn't want to jump up, make his excuses and leave, break the intimate silence with meaningless small talk designed to keep a clear distance between his companion and himself. He wanted to stay here, holding Lawrie Bennett, and just *be*.

Although he really ought to think about getting dressed. He had been to this cove many times, and had yet to see another living soul beyond the gulls, but there was always a first time, and he'd rather not be naked when that time came. He ran a hand along the length of Lawrie's body, shoulder to hip, feeling the slight curves, marvelling at the silkiness of her skin. Even now, unclothed, half-asleep, there was a quiet dignity to her—a dignity that had been noticeable by its absence during the last hour.

He smiled to himself as he ran his hand back up her body, feeling her quiver under his touch. Passionate, unguarded, fiery, tender—she had been many things but not dignified.

'Lawrie?'

'Hmm?'

'Wake up, honey, it's getting late.'

She muttered something indistinguishable, rolling over away from him. He flicked his eyes down her graceful back, lingering at her curved behind, before trying again.

'Come on, Lawrie, time to get dressed. You wouldn't want some ramblers copping an eyeful, would you? Though it'd probably make their day—do wonders for the local tourist economy.'

She muttered again but rolled back, pushing herself up until she was sitting, legs drawn close to her chest as she flicked her hair out of her still sleepy eyes. 'What time is it?'

He held up his bare arm. 'No watch…no phone,' he teased. 'Can you cope with being so far from communication and order?'

She smiled, but warily. 'Good thing I brought

my bag,' she said. 'I think I should probably get dressed, though. Erm…could you possibly…?' She gestured at her clothes, neatly folded on top of the rock.

'Of course,' he said, getting to his feet and noticing how her eyes were drawn towards his body before she lowered them, a faint blush staining her cheeks. Taking pity, he threw her shorts and T-shirt to her before retrieving his, unable to keep from watching her as she wriggled into her clothes in as discreet a style as possible.

'Don't mind me,' he said, and grinned as her head came up and she glared at him.

'A gentleman would turn his back.'

'Poor gentleman—he'd miss out.'

She stood up slowly, stretching out her arms and legs with a lithe grace. 'Do you want a hand?' She gestured at the blanket and towels.

'Do you want to rush off? I brought food and wine.'

She eyed him nervously. 'You said it was getting late, that we should get back.'

'It is, and we should,' he agreed. 'But we can stay a little longer if you want—or do you have plans tonight?'

'No, but if I drink that I won't be able to drive home,' she pointed out as he reached into the rucksack and drew out a bottle of wine encased in a cooling holder.

'I own a hotel. Finding a bed for the night is never a problem.' He unscrewed the top and handed it to her. 'You're not too posh to drink from the bottle, are you?'

'Seriously?'

Her face spoke volumes but at his amused nod she screwed up her nose and raised the bottle to her lips. Only Lawrie Bennett could make drinking from a bottle look refined. And sexy.

'I, however, don't own a hotel.'

'We may have a spare tent somewhere—*ow!*' This as she flicked his shoulder smartly. 'What was that for?'

'Seriously, Jonas. What are you suggesting? That I stay at the hotel tonight with you? People are already talking...' Her voice trailed off.

'So what?' People always talked. They'd been talking since the second she'd sashayed back into town. Let them. 'Come and eat something. I brought all of this for you. I'm not lugging it back up the cliff.'

Lawrie flopped down onto the blanket next to him and took the paper plate he was holding out to her, loading it daintily with a selection of breads, cheeses and salads. She began to build a towering sandwich of cheese, salad, grapes and coleslaw.

Jonas watched, fascinated. 'That's quite some sandwich,' he said.

'Hmm, I'm not quite sure how I'm going to manage to bite into it,' she admitted. 'Maybe sandwiches could be my thing?'

'What thing?'

'Well, you said it yourself—I'm a blender. I don't have an interest that's really mine,' she said, reassembling the sandwich into several smaller parts. 'Maybe it's time I did. In New York they asked me what I liked to do in my spare time and I told them about going to museums and exhibitions. But of course that was Hugo's interest, not mine. I enjoyed them, but would I go by myself? And then I said singing, but I only do that when I'm with you. I don't know *what* I like to do apart from work.'

'And sandwich-making is your new hobby?'

'Being a foodie might be. I've had a lot of practice. Or I might take up art? What?' she asked as he shook his head.

'I've played Pictionary with you. Believe me when I say that art is *not* your thing.'

'Good point. Well, maybe quilting, or distressing furniture.'

'You could… But you don't have to decide right now, do you?'

'But if I decide before I go then I can research,' she said, taking a bite of the newly assembled sandwich. She chewed, then swallowed. 'I'll tell you what I'm not going to do, though. I am not going to date anyone I work with. Especially not my boss. Twice bitten, three times shy. Or something.'

Jonas grinned. 'Interesting statement, considering I am kind of your boss now.' His smile grew wider, more wicked, as he saw the blush colour her pale cheeks, the answering smile in her eyes. 'And, considering how you've been spending your nights lately, I have to conclude that you haven't started to enforce that rule too strictly.'

She laughed and her colour was high, her lips reddening, full, inviting. 'Ah, but we're not dating.'

'No?'

'No.'

'Then…' He leant in, close. Took her hand in his, turning it over to slowly trace a circle on her palm. 'What *are* we doing late at night, Miss Bennett?'

She swayed towards him, her hand closing onto his. Jonas slid his thumb over the plump flesh of her palm, every sense suddenly heightened. The brightness of the sun illuminated the scene in honey-coloured light: her glorious hair, the creaminess of her skin, the crash of the waves onto the shoreline, the call of the birds swooping high above, the distant coconut smell of gorse mingling with her light, fresh perfume, the silky smoothness of her hands in his. The anticipation of taste. The so very sweet anticipation…

He pulled her closer, sliding his hands out of hers and up her bare arms, then down her back, where they rested on the soft skin of her shoulderblades. His thumbs moved in small circles. She shivered under his touch, her breath speeding up, coming in small gasps, as one finger slid leisurely down her spine and then up to the nape of her neck. She swayed towards him, her face tilted up, eyelids half closed, desire and need in her expression, her eyes, her mouth. He leant in, brushed her mouth with his oh, so slowly, before trailing kisses along her jaw, down the side of her neck, to the soft pulse beating insistently in her throat.

She sighed, leaning against him as his tongue flicked out, tasted her warm skin. His hands were still playing up and down her spine, enjoying her uninhibited response to his touch, his kiss, the feel of her quivering beneath him.

'Jonas…' she began, one hand coming up to clutch his T-shirt, the other to encircle his neck.

But whatever she'd been going to say was interrupted by the shrillness of a ringtone from her bag, flung carelessly at his feet. Lawrie pulled back slowly, her expression clearing, releasing him. Reluctantly he let her go, his hand lingering against her back as he did so.

She gave him an apologetic smile. 'I should get this.'

Jonas nodded, standing up and taking a step away to recover himself as she rooted in her bag and pulled out the insistently shrieking phone.

He closed his eyes, inhaling the sea air deeply. He felt so alive. At some point in the last few days

his eagerness for life, his zest, had returned—
and yet he hadn't even noticed that it was gone

'Yes…yes. Absolutely. That sounds great—
thank you. Yes, okay. I will. Bye.' Lawrie switched
the phone off and stood still, a dazed expression
on her face.

He looked over at her enquiringly. 'Bad news?'

'Huh? Oh, no.' She looked a little dazed. 'No,
it was the agency.' A wide smile broke out on her
face. 'The New York firm want me! They were
really impressed with my interview and want
me to start the day my gardening leave finishes.
Isn't it wonderful?'

'Yes, wonderful.' Jonas forced a smile onto
his face, made himself move over to her, pull
her close into a hug. 'Of course they want you.
They'd be mad not to.'

She returned the embrace, then stepped back,
excitement filling her vivid dark eyes. 'New
York…' Her face glowed. 'It's all coming together, Jonas.'

'Of course it is. You've made it come together.'

She had. She'd worked hard for it, picked herself up when it all had been snatched away from
her. She deserved this.

So why did it feel as if the bottom had dropped out of his world?

'So?' She was tugging at his hand, playfully. 'You were saying before we were interrupted...?'

'I think we should head back,' he said, still with that forced smile on his face. 'News like this calls for champagne.'

She looked slightly surprised, a little disappointed, but didn't demur, helping him pack up, chattering about New York, the firm, the work she hoped to be doing. He listened, agreed, asked questions, and the topic lasted them all the way home.

Her eyes were firmly fixed on the bright lights of a big city once again.

CHAPTER TEN

THE FIELDS WERE full of life. Families, couples, groups of friends, were laughing, chattering, wandering into one of the myriad teepees, tents and yurts to enjoy theatre, storytelling, music or poetry readings. Food stalls offered local beers and ciders, and every type of food, from traditional Cornish cream teas to Indian street food. Meanwhile over on the main stage one of Cornwall's best-known folk bands was entertaining a large crowd. It was exhausting. It was exhilarating. Lawrie was loving every minute of it.

When she had a chance to stop and think about it, that was.

She reached up a hand to check the earpiece that kept her connected to the main radio network bleating out security breaches, lost children, petty theft, missing artists. She was aware of every single incident taking place on the festival site. Even last night, when she'd stayed in

Jonas's camper van, parked backstage so she was in the midst of the activity at all times, she'd kept it switched on. Her bulging file and her phone had been close by the bed, ready to be snatched up at a moment's notice.

She hadn't slept a wink.

But here they were: Day Two. The sun was still miraculously shining, no musician so lost he couldn't be found and shoved out on stage on time, every sobbing child reunited with grateful parents. No food poisoning—yet, she thought anxiously—no serious crimes or marauding youths. Just a happy, laid-back vibe. Like a swan, with the festival-goers the body, floating serenely along, whilst she and the other members of staff paddled furiously to keep the whole thing afloat.

Goodness, what an overblown simile. She must be tired.

'When did you last eat?'

She jumped as a pair of hands landed on her shoulders, squeezing lightly.

'Have you even sat down once in the last two days?' Jonas continued mock severely. 'Taken time to listen to one of the bands you booked?'

'They were mostly booked before I started,' she

protested, resisting the urge to lean back against him, to surrender the worries, the responsibilities into his oh, so capable hands for just a few seconds.

'It's on; we're live; it's all good,' he said, turning her round to face him. 'You should relax and start enjoying it.'

Lawrie hugged the black file that had been her constant companion over the last month closer to her chest. 'I'll enjoy it in twenty-four hours' time,' she told him. 'Once I know the last bands have turned up and that tonight has run smoothly.'

'Or once you've picked the last piece of litter up from the campsite in a week's time?'

She smiled. 'Maybe.'

Like her, Jonas was dressed casually. There was no sign of the successful businessman in the cut-off denims and orange T-shirt, a baseball cap covering the blond hair subtracting years from him.

'Well, at least let me buy you some lunch.'

'I'm not really hungry,' she demurred.

But, too tired to make a fuss, she allowed him to lead her to a falafel stand and order her a humus salad wrap. The smell of fried onions and spicy chickpeas hit her as she stood there; they smelt like summer. A hollow feeling in her stomach reminded her that actually she had barely touched her breakfast that morning, nor supper the night before.

'Part of the fun of Wave Fest is the food,' he scolded her as she nibbled at the edges of the wrap, trying to avoid spilling what was inside down her top. 'You should be getting out there, experimenting.'

She licked humus off the top of the wrap. 'I'm not really the experimenting type.'

He leant in close. 'I don't agree.'

His breath tickled her ear, soft, tantalising, like a soft summer breeze. The faint brush of air on her sensitive earlobe spread through her body, warming her right down to her toes. She was almost paralysed with a sudden stab of desire—hotter, needier, more intense than ever. She swallowed, willing her knees to stay up, her stomach to settle, trying to control her traitorous body. It was the hunger, the lack of sleep, the craziness of the day. She couldn't still want him—not this much.

Her time here was almost over.

The thought was a short, sharp shock. The sweet, languorous need that had enveloped her fled as quickly as it had come. Their time together was nearly at an end—as it should be... as she wanted.

Autumn was coming. By the time the leaves had turned she would be across the ocean, beginning her new life. Jonas would be here.

They both knew long-distance didn't work. They had failed so spectacularly before.

Lawrie plastered a bright smile on her face, turning to look at him, hoping that no trace of her thoughts remained visible.

'Have you seen many of the bands?' she asked, before taking a bite of the wrap. She nearly moaned out loud. Maybe it *was* lack of food that had caused her earlier weakness, because the combination of crisp wrap, rocket, humus and freshly made falafal was sensual overload.

'Is that good?'

Amusement was written all over his face as she nodded mutely, cramming another mouthful in.

'Maybe I was hungry,' she mumbled as she swallowed it down.

'Maybe.' His eyes were bright with laughter. 'You'll be admitting you need a nap next.'

She shook her head. 'Try coffee—caffeine might help,' she allowed.

He took her elbow, steering her effortlessly through the partying crowds. 'At least come into the hotel and sit down while you drink it,' he said, and the thought of a comfy armchair was too tempting.

She allowed him to lead her away, finishing off the wrap hungrily as they walked back to the hotel.

'Are your parents still here?' she asked as they mounted the steps and made their way through the crowded foyer to the desk. The hotel itself was strictly VIP for the duration of the festival, but it was no less hectic than outside, with staff, guests and the bands not camping backstage all based there.

'No, they left after a seafood lunch.'

His voice was non-committal. She sneaked a peep at his face but it was expressionless. Her heart sank. Getting his parents to agree to visit the hotel during the festival had seemed like a major coup; she hoped it hadn't backfired.

'That's a shame,' she said carefully. 'I would have liked to see them again.'

'Maybe it's for the best.' He flashed her a warm smile. 'My mother, despite thinking that you are far, far too good for me, has not-so-secret hopes that we may get back together and she can have her dream daughter-in-law again. Don't worry— I warned her that you're off again soon.'

He could at least sound a little regretful about it.

If only she wasn't so tired, could think more clearly. Where was that coffee?

She followed Jonas into her office and curled up thankfully on the large squishy sofa.

He cast her a concerned look. 'You are done in.'

'Not at all,' she protested. 'A coffee will sort me out.'

He looked unconvinced, but made her promise not to try and get up, no matter what, and then disappeared off to fetch her a drink. Lawrie leant back against the cool, plumped-up cushions and sighed. She *had* hoped that seeing the festival in full swing would help his parents appreciate all that Jonas had achieved, but maybe she'd been wrong.

Maybe she needed to accept that some things were best left alone. If she had kept to her original plan and stayed clear of Jonas then she would be in such a different frame of mind as she contemplated her life changing move.

She sighed. She should be much more excited, optimistic. This was what she wanted.

And yet it was as if her life had been beige and grey for the past nine years and colour had suddenly returned to it. It was bright, and it hurt sometimes, but oh, the difference it madc. She just had to figure out how to keep the Technicolor when she left. When she started again.

'I managed to get you carrot cake as well.' Jonas returned to the room, carefully carrying a tray holding a cafetière of deliciously pungent coffee and a large slab of spicily fragrant sponge cake. 'Sugar and caffeine should sort you out.'

He placed the tray onto the small coffee table and poured out a cup of coffee, adding cream and handing it over to Lawrie, who sniffed ecstatically.

'I can't believe you've got me addicted to coffee again,' she said accusingly as she took a sip of the bitter brew.

'You are moving to New York,' he pointed out as he poured a cup for himself and sat next to her on the sofa. 'You don't want to be seen as a strange tea-drinking Brit who spends the whole time complaining that she can't get a proper brew, do you?'

'Well, no,' she conceded, leaning forward to hook the plate of cake off the tray. She forked a small portion of frosting and sponge and sat looking at it for a second.

'Are you going to eat that or just study it?'

'Eat it,' she retorted, and suited her action to her words.

She sucked the fork appreciatively, her mind still whirling.

'Did you serve them the shellfish special or the fried fish platter?' She attempted to keep her tone light, nonchalant, and licked the last bit of frosting off the cake fork.

'Huh?'

Jonas's eyes were glued to the fork, to her tongue flicking out and licking it. She coloured, forking up some more cake casually, as if she hadn't noticed his intense gaze, the disconcerting gleam in the blue eyes.

'Your parents? I think they're more shellfish people myself, but the whitebait on the fried platter is so delicious.' She was on the verge of babbling, but her words had the desired effect. Jonas pulled his eyes away from her mouth distractedly.

'My parents? Oh, the shellfish. They like big, extravagant gestures so it had to be lobster, really.'

'And did they see any bands?'

'Oh, yes. They had the full guided tour.'

'And...?' she prompted him.

He gave her a rueful grin. 'They didn't throw themselves on my neck with tears of apology for neglecting me all these years and promises of a brighter tomorrow,' he said.

His words were light, almost jocular, without the slight undercurrent of disappointment or the hint of bitterness talk of his parents usually brought out in him.

'On the other hand they didn't criticise, cry with disappointment or walk out in disgust. They stayed for lunch and even said it was "rather nice" so overall a success, I think.'

'A complete success,' she agreed.

He reached out his hand, tucking back a lock of her hair. She sat frozen, aware of nothing but his touch, the unexpectedly tender look in his eyes, the sound of her own heartbeat hammering.

Their eyes continued to hold. Her mouth was dry, she flicked her tongue out nervously to moisten her lips. They had been alone, been intimate, so many times—every night for the last few weeks—but this...this felt different. It felt *more*. But even as part of her welcomed it, thirsted for it, another, larger part of her shrank from it. It was too much.

Because they had been here before.

'I should go.' Was that really her voice? So hesitant, so unsure? She pushed herself up, legs wobbly. 'Wave Fest won't run itself, you know.'

He was still seated, still looking at her with that disconcertingly knowing gaze, as if he could see right inside her. He was so close. He just needed to reach out, pull, and she would be in his lap.

But if she allowed herself to settle there she would never want to leave.

He didn't. Didn't move, didn't pull, didn't try and dissuade her. He just watched her as she drank down the rest of her coffee, grabbed her file and walked out of the office. He didn't say a word.

* * *

Work. It was always the answer. And this was a workaholic's dream. The second she left the office Lawrie was pounced upon to sort out some problem with the evening's line-up, and by the time she'd pacified the disgruntled artist who expected a higher billing she'd managed to push all thoughts of Jonas to the back of her mind— where, she told herself sternly, he had better stay until she felt more like herself again.

Whatever and whoever herself might be. She certainly wasn't the brittle London girl who had arrived here just over a month ago, but she wasn't the Cornish girl in vest top and shorts she appeared to be either. She was only playing at her role here.

But, playing or not, there was a lot to do.

Eight hours later her lunch was just a distant dream. She had barely had the opportunity to grab any water, despite the heat of the sun, and must have walked miles. Next year she would recommend golf carts, she thought.

'There you are.'

Lawrie turned around, blinked blearily. Everything was suddenly amplified. The light was almost blinding; people and objects were a mingled blur. The sounds were an amalgamated cacophony of discordant notes and loud voices.

She swayed, pressing a trembling hand to her head.

'Lawrie! Are you okay?'

Jonas. How broad he looked…how comforting. She took a small step towards him, then stopped, trying to summon up the energy to reply. 'Yes, just tired still. I'll be fine.'

It had been such a warm day. And yet now she was shaking with cold, wrapping her arms around herself, trying to press some warmth into her bones.

A touch on her chin tilted it upwards. She tried to meet his probing gaze but had to close her eyes.

'I told you to take a proper rest. There are another twenty-four hours of this festival, and you are not going to last,' Jonas said grimly and, disregarding her protests, whirled around, taking her elbow and pulling her along.

'What are you doing?' she said, trying unsuccessfully to pull her arm out of his grasp.

'Taking you home for the night. If you are on

site you won't switch off,' he said pulling out his handset. 'Fliss, you are in charge for the next twelve hours. Lawrie is taking a few hours off.'

Lawrie could hear Fliss's voice floating up from the handset, worrying, agreeing, admonishing Lawrie to get some rest.

She wanted to argue, to tell them she was fine but the words wouldn't come. 'Are you all ganging up on me?'

'If that's what it takes.'

She felt as if she should fight harder but she didn't have the strength. 'Just a short nap,' she conceded.

'You are having the whole night off. You can come back tomorrow morning, but not a second before.' There was no trace of humour in his voice, just worry. 'And I'll see how you are then.'

'Yes, boss.'

But it was an effort to form the words, and she didn't demur as Jonas led her through the crowds and round to the staff car park, where he gently helped her into his car.

Lawrie sank into the seat and closed her eyes. Half asleep, she didn't notice the route Jonas took until he stopped the car with an undignified squeal of brakes. She prised her eyelids open and looked about her. They were in the tiny old town, amongst the fishermen's cottages that clustered around the harbour.

'This isn't home,' she murmured sleepily.

'This is my house,' Jonas told her, and he unbuckled her seat belt before getting out and coming round to open her door and help her out. 'I don't trust you not to be logging on and fussing if I let you go back to yours.'

'Too tired to log on,' she protested, but obediently followed him along the street.

They were at the very top of the old town, with the cliffs towering above them and views over the rooftops down to the harbour below. Jonas came to a stop by a long crooked house that lurched drunkenly along the street and opened the door. Lawrie stopped on the doorstep and stared at him, suddenly more awake.

'The crooked house? You bought it?'

'Yep. Come in.'

She looked at him. Didn't he remember? That this was *the house*—the one that every time they played the 'one day when we are rich' game they had decided they would buy. Some were bigger, others more imposing, cuter, older, quainter, but something about this last house in the old town had appealed to her the most. The funny little corners, the different levels, the roof garden… It had always drawn her in, and now it belonged to Jonas.

'Lawrie, are you all right?'

'Yes, I'm coming.'

Slowly she stepped into her dream house. Inside it was just as she'd imagined. The hall that bisected the mismatched halves of the house was covered in grey flagstones, a wooden bannister curved around the crooked staircase.

She didn't have time to see more as Jonas ushered her straight upstairs. He turned down the winding passage to his left and stopped at the first door, pausing with his hand on the handle, a look of slight embarrassment on his face. 'I haven't made the other beds up but my sheets are clean on…' He trailed off.

She stared at him incredulously, then laughed. 'Jonas, we have been sleeping together most nights for the last month—plus, I am so tired I wouldn't care if your sheets hadn't been changed in weeks.'

He grinned. 'Good point,' he said and, turning the handle, ushered her inside.

It was a large, rectangular room, with two small windows cut into the deep walls, the stone window seats covered in plush cushions. An oak bedstead dominated the room and was made up in a rich, dark chocolate linen. It was the most inviting thing Lawrie had ever seen.

'Right…' He still stood at the door. 'I will leave you to…ah…make yourself comfortable. There's a bathroom just there.' He gestured at a door set in the far wall. 'I'll be back in the morning with some clean clothes and a meal, so just sleep, okay?'

''kay…' She nodded, but her eyes were already fixated on the plump, cool-looking pillows, the king-size comfortable bed.

Jonas had scarcely pulled the door shut behind him before she'd started to undress, kicking off her shoes, slipping off her shorts and unhooking her bra, manoeuvring it off under her vest top. Clad just in her top and knickers, she climbed into the bed and closed her eyes.

As she drifted off to sleep the events of the day replayed themselves. Why had Jonas been so funny about her sleeping in his bed? Of *course*, she thought drowsily as sleep began to overtake her. They had only shared a bed to have sex—sometimes sleeping together afterwards, sometimes he would leave her and go home. But this—this letting her into his bed, into his home—this was intimacy.

It scared her...it comforted her.

Lawrie drifted off to sleep.

It wasn't worth going back to the hotel, Jonas decided. After all, Fliss could cope for a few hours, and if she couldn't he was just fifteen minutes' drive away; it could take longer than that to walk from one side of the site to the other.

Dropping by Lawrie's to pick her up a change of clothes had taken him far longer than he'd anticipated. Choosing an outfit had felt almost uncomfortably intimate—which, considering some of the truly intimate actions he had been performing with and to her on a nightly basis, was just too weird.

He hadn't wanted to dwell on why that might be, choosing a dress and cardigan almost at random and plucking underwear out of her drawer with his face averted.

Well, maybe he'd had a little peek. But not a long one—he wasn't one of *those* guys.

Back at his house, he wandered into his sitting room, falling onto the leather corner sofa with a sigh, his mind fixated on the room above, where Lawrie slept. He had avoided bringing her here, to his home, to the house she had once loved so much.

He dragged his eyes away from the ceiling he was staring at as if he had X-ray vision—as if he could see through to the room, to the bed, to the sleeping girl above—fixing his gaze instead on the large watercolour portrait that hung above the open fireplace. It was a sea scene, of course—every work of art he owned reflected the coast in some way—in which a girl sat on a rock, staring out to a wild sea, her hair whipped and blowing. She was turned away from the artist, so only a small part of her face could be seen.

Lawrie. A portrait painted by a summer visitor years ago. Jonas had tracked it down and bought it several years ago.

He didn't really like to examine his reasons why. Just as he didn't like to examine his reasons for buying this house in particular. The house he and Lawrie had play-furnished in their dreams time and time again. He could easily afford something bigger, fancier, more luxurious, but he felt grounded here—at home.

In the house she'd loved, with her portrait on the wall.

He sat bolt upright, adrenaline running through him. What was he *doing*? What had he been doing these last nine years?

He was pathetic. All these years he had prided himself on how independent he was, how he needed no one but himself, and look at him.

No wonder he was still single. How could any real woman compete with the ghost at the feast? They had never had a chance, had they? No matter how fun or accomplished or sexy they were, they had always been missing something very important.

They weren't Lawrie.

Maybe part of him had held on, hoping for her

return. And here she was. Back in his life and back in his bed.

About to leave again.

He could try and change her mind. He could ask her to stay, beg her to stay. Rush up there now and tell her how he felt.

And then what?

Jonas got to his feet and walked over to the painting. There she was, her eyes fixed on the horizon, on the future. She had always dreamt big.

Right now she was vulnerable, more scarred by the loss of her job and her fiancé than she would ever admit. He could play on that fear and she might stay.

And then what?

He knew too well how *that* scenario played out. He would watch her feel more and more confined and constricted. Watch her start to blame and resent him. Again. Watch her walk away, walk out of his life, and this time never come back.

Or he could let her go and then move on himself. Finally, *properly* move on.

He looked at the clock sitting on the mantelpiece. Eight hours before he needed to wake her. It wouldn't hurt if he just stretched out for a while himself. The sofa was long enough, wide enough, comfortable enough… And yet he couldn't relax.

This was ridiculous. He had a perfectly good bed upstairs. Lawrie wouldn't mind.

She was fast asleep, the covers kicked off, exposing long, lean legs. The curve of her bottom encased in sheer black silk was a stark contrast to the cream of her skin. The strap of her vest had fallen down, showing a rare vulnerability in the usually self-possessed, contained, organised Lawrie. Looking down at her, he felt a tenderness creep over him for his beautiful, intelligent wife.

Ex-wife. Just two letters made such a difference.

Jonas kicked off his shoes and quietly slipped his shorts off, hanging them on the chair before crossing the room to get into bed beside her. He fitted his length against her, pulling her in close, one arm holding her tight.

'I love you,' he whispered. 'I'll always love you.'

Eyes open, thoughts racing, Jonas lay there, holding Lawrie close, willing time to slow, wishing that the night would last for ever.

CHAPTER ELEVEN

IT WAS THE campfire's fault. If Lawrie hadn't attended the end-of-festival campfire—hadn't met up with old friends, hadn't found herself singing songs she had forgotten she had ever known, hadn't cooed over babies and admired stroppy, tired toddlers, hadn't met new couples and heard one hundred stories about how they'd met…

If she hadn't spent the evening watching Jonas, golden in the flickering firelight, laughing, relaxing, looking over at her with laughter, with tenderness in his eyes.

If after the campfire they hadn't sneaked back to the camper van. If they hadn't made love with an intensity she couldn't remember having ever experienced before.

She should have left the minute the festival finished—packed her bags and disappeared without a word.

Then she wouldn't need to find the words to say goodbye. Find the will to turn and walk away.

'You're very quiet.'

Jonas was once more driving her to the airport.

Only this time there would be no return trip.

She forced a smile. 'I'm a little apprehensive,' she admitted.

He raised an eyebrow. 'Lawrie Bennett, lawyer, festival-organiser, campfire chanteuse…apprehensive? I don't believe it.'

He was so calm, so *cheerful*. As if her leaving didn't matter at all.

And, although she couldn't handle a scene, a little regret might be nice—a sign that their time together had meant something to him.

What if he asked you to stay?

Where had that thought come from?

She pushed it to one side, searching for something to say. 'Do you think I'm like my mother?'

As soon as she asked the question she regretted it, not sure she could bear to hear the answer.

Jonas looked surprised. That was good, right?

'I can't imagine you abandoning your teenage daughter while you go and party in Goa, no,' he said finally. 'Why?'

Immediately Lawrie wanted to backtrack. What could she tell him? That she wasn't sure about leaving? Didn't know if she could do this alone?

She fell back on an old conversation. 'I don't even know what I like, for goodness' sake. Is festival-going, shorts-wearing, beach-loving Lawrie more real than the suited and booted City lawyer? I worry that I'm a chameleon, Jonas, just like she is.'

Excuse it might be, but there was truth there. She had always defended her need to blend in. Maybe it was time to learn to stand out.

He was silent for a moment. 'Your mother spent her life searching—you've spent yours *doing*. You have spent your life trying to achieve something, Law. You have been working for it since I knew you. You're dedicated, single-minded. That's nothing like her. You never wasted your time on dreams and fairytales.'

That was true, but not enough. 'But I don't even know whether I like the stuff I like because of me, or because of you or Hugo. See? Chameleon!'

He laughed, and the warm humour caressed her taut nerves.

'We're back to this, are we?'

She nodded, slightly shame-faced.

'You're not a chameleon, I promise. Maybe you've just found it easier to adapt to other people's interests as that gives you more time to concentrate on what really matters to you.'

He was silent for a moment, concentrating on overtaking, and Lawrie took his words in, a warmth stealing over as she did so.

He understood her. In some ways better than she understood herself.

He spoke again, quiet and serious. 'For what it's worth, I think you're both of those people. Even city slickers are allowed to be beach bums occasionally. You don't have to choose. Okay— we're here.'

Looking up with a start, Lawrie realised Jonas was taking a left hand turn—the one that led to the airport short-stay car park. He was planning to come in.

Panic clawed at her chest. She couldn't handle a long, protracted goodbye. Memories flashed through her of tearful train station farewells, clutching desperately on to Jonas as the train drew in, suitcase at her feet.

She'd never been good at goodbyes.

'You don't need to stay, honestly. Just drop me off.'

He flashed her a quick glance. 'You sure?'

She put on her brightest smile. 'Goodness, yes. You don't want to waste an hour hanging out at the airport, and I don't have much luggage—most of my stuff was shipped out last week. I'll head straight to the departure lounge and read there. You go.'

There was a slightly desperate tinge to her voice as she finished speaking but Jonas didn't seem to notice—he just turned the car around to drive into the drop-off area.

He pulled up to the kerb and they sat there. Silent. Lawrie stared at her hands, twisting them nervously together.

'Okay, then, this is it.'

'Yep.'

'I'll get your bag.'

Once again he was walking round the car to fetch her bag. Once again she was sliding out of the low-slung seats, stepping onto the grey paving slabs, ready to walk through the sliding glass doors.

Once again she was leaving.

'Right—you have your suitcase, laptop, handbag, jacket, tickets, passport?'

She nodded. 'I'm all good.'

'Okay, then.' He was moving away, the few steps back towards the car. It was just Lawrie and her bags, alone on the pavement. Just as she wanted. *Fight me on this,* she thought desperately. *Come in with me. See me off. Ask me not to go.*

The need was getting louder, harder to ignore.

Lawrie picked up her bag, testing its weight. This was it. She shot a look over at him, leaning against the bonnet, oblivious or uncaring of the cars lined up behind, waiting for a drop-off spot. His face was calm, set. Inscrutable.

'Law...?'

She paused, a fizz of hope bubbling up inside her, shocking her with its intensity.

'Just remember: tea is drunk hot, not iced, and jelly wobbles and is always eaten with ice cream.'

And just like that she was flat.

She attempted a smile. 'I thought you wanted me to fit in?'

'Fit in? Yes. Go native? No.'

The world had fallen away. All she was aware

of was him. The foot between them seemed an ocean already—that solid, comforting presence a continent away. It was up to her. Only her.

And it terrified her.

Lawrie took a deep breath. 'I could stay if you wanted me to. If you asked me I would consider it, definitely.' *Ask me,* she begged silently. *Tell me you need me...you can't live without me. Tell me it will be better this time. Tell me we can make it.*

His expression didn't change. 'Why?'

Lawrie didn't know what she had expected him to do. To regretfully but politely turn her down and send her on her way? To run over to her, swoop her up, twirl her, like a montage of every rom-com she had seen? To be embarrassed?

But she hadn't expected that one-word question. She hadn't expected the warm blue eyes to turn to steel.

'Last-minute nerves,' she said as brightly as she could, pulling the tattered shreds of her pride around her, trying to match his cool expression. 'You know I hate saying goodbye. It's been a good few weeks. I got carried away, sorry. Forget I said anything.'

'What if I did ask?'

How could she have thought him calm? His voice reverberated with suppressed emotion. But not the emotion she'd hoped for. It wasn't warm, comforting, loving.

'Would you make it till the end of the year? Till next summer? How long before you blame me because you're stuck here and not in New York?'

Wow. Lawrie had never really believed that words could hurt before, but that hit deep—painfully deep. 'I can't believe you said that…' she almost whispered, torn between hot tears and plain old-fashioned anger. 'I only asked you…'

'You asked me to make a decision for you. *Again.* You want to stay, Lawrie?' The words whipped through the air, taut and clear. 'You stay. *You* make the decision and *you* live with the consequences. Don't ask somebody else to shoulder the responsibility for you so you can blame them the second it goes wrong.'

'I'm not!' All her verbal skills had deserted her. She was defenceless against the unexpected onslaught.

'No?' His laugh had no humour in it. 'You didn't blame me for keeping you here before? For getting married so young?'

The warmth of the summer's day had disappeared and a chill wind goosepimpled her bare arms, making her shiver. 'We were young!'

'You said yourself you would still be with your ex, making wedding plans, if he hadn't forced your hand. Now you want me to force it again?' Jonas shook his head. 'I don't think so, Lawrie. Take some responsibility for yourself, decide what the hell you want—what you *really* want—and then maybe we can talk.'

'I don't need to talk.' Lawrie's uncertainty and shock had disappeared, been replaced with a burning anger. How dared he speak to her like that? 'I made a mistake. Clearly. Thanks for pointing that out. Message received.'

And, picking up her bag, she turned and strode away as confidently as she could, his steel-blue gaze burning into her back as she did so.

No one had warned her how cold New York could be. It was barely autumn—fall, she corrected herself—and already the temperatures were dropping, the wind was howling through the island city, and the rain lashed down in great dramatic storms.

Not that Lawrie had much time to concentrate on the weather. New York prided itself on being the city that never slept and its standards were high. She was no shirker, but it was taking everything just to keep up.

And keeping up wasn't enough. She needed to excel. Others might skate in Central Park, go for coffee wrapped up in giant jumpers and cashmere scarves and hats; Lawrie worked. She had found a small studio flat close to the office, but spent so much time at her desk it really was just a base to sleep, shower and eat. Ostensibly she was apartment-hunting, looking for a place of her own to buy. In reality her attempts mirrored her wedding-planning with Hugo. Non-existent.

Hugo was now married to his secretary, Helen—happily, she assumed. His social media pages certainly painted that picture, showing a beaming Hugo—he had put on weight, she thought critically—with one arm possessively around his blooming bride. Every detail of Helen's pregnancy was detailed, along with scans, possible baby names and more information about her physical symptoms than Lawrie was entirely comfortable with.

On the surface she was cynically amused, but buried deep down inside—*very* deep down—she was touched and a little jealous. Not of Helen and Hugo, exactly, but of the absolute patent happiness that glowed out of every sentimental update. No amount of completed contracts, of senior partner compliments could compete with that.

And Jonas didn't get in touch. Not one word. No apology.

And she didn't contact him.

His last words reverberated around her mind, echoing at unexpected times. Not just when she was alone, and not just in the dead of night as she lay sleepless in an unfamiliar bed in a strange city, but in meetings, at the gym, as she walked down the street.

Take some responsibility.

And then the anger flared up again, but it was getting weaker as the days slowly passed.

And at the same time that unwanted voice was whispering insistently, *What if you could do it again? Would you ask him or would you tell him? Would you tell him you were staying and want to be with him?*

Would you tell him that you love him?

* * *

'Are you having a party this year?'

Jonas looked up irritably. 'What?'

'I asked,' Fliss repeated equably, 'if you want to have a birthday party again this year?'

As Jonas's birthday coincided with the final weekend of the season—the start of autumn proper—he usually had a big party at the Boat House. A chance for the locals and the villagers to let their hair down and reclaim their home after months of incomers.

He couldn't imagine anything worse, but the speculation if he missed a year would be unbearable.

'I haven't really thought about it. I suppose so.'

'Oh, great!' Fliss was obviously annoyed. 'Masses of preparation for "I suppose so". What you mean is, *Thank you, Fliss, I would love to— and, yes, I will of course be leaving the grumpy expression and the grunting at home and try to enjoy myself for once in my miserable life.*'

That was a little too close for comfort. 'That's enough,' he snapped.

Fliss looked anxious. 'Honestly, Jonas, you've been the proverbial sore-headed bear for weeks.

Even *I* am finding you pretty difficult, and I have a much higher Jonas tolerance than most.'

Jonas swung his chair round and stared at her. 'Oh, come on. I know I've been a bit short—'

'A *bit*?' she interjected.

'Busy—'

'A reclusive workaholic.'

'And I don't suffer fools gladly.' He shot her a look as she opened her mouth and she snapped it shut. 'There has been a lot happening, as I am sure you have noticed: new cafés, two new hotels, getting the clothes line launch ready for next year.'

'I know,' she said. 'I work here too, remember?'

'Well, then, life isn't all surfing. Sometimes it is pure, hard, exhausting work.'

'But a balance is always good. When did you last take a board out? Not since the day after Lawrie left.'

'Don't say her name!'

It was involuntary, and he cursed himself for revealing so much—for revealing everything. But Fliss didn't look shocked or horrified. She looked knowing. She looked…heck…she looked *sorry* for him. Jonas gritted his teeth.

'Just because L… Because her departure coincided with a busy period does not mean that my present mood has anything to do with her.'

Fliss looked apologetic. 'But we've been here before,' she reminded him. 'That summer she left, before the third Wave Fest, you changed. You went curt and mean and nearly drove all your staff away. You worked twenty-four-seven and a year later—*voilà*—five more cafés and a mini-chain.'

'And a career for you.'

'And a career for me,' she agreed. 'But I bloody earned it, Jonas. And I am earning it now, acting as a buffer between you and the staff, trying to keep up with your breakneck speed, going along with the vision whilst making sure that we don't over-expand—and that we don't lose all our staff while we do so.'

His voice was icy. 'I know what I'm doing.'

'Well, yes, we all know what you're doing. You're throwing yourself into work to forget about Lawrie. After all, it worked once before. Is it working now?'

Not really. His mouth twisted. 'She wanted me

to ask her to stay.' The words were out before he could stop them.

Fliss didn't look surprised 'Did you?'

Jonas stared at Fliss. 'No,' he said bleakly. 'No, I told her to go.'

'Why?'

The same question he'd asked Lawrie. The question that had swept the hope out of her eyes and left her looking broken.

He shook his head, trying to clear her stricken face from his mind. 'Because it's not my decision to make. If she wanted to be with me she would. I shouldn't need to ask.'

'Jonas, I love you, and I love her too, but you— you're my best mate as well as my boss and I'm worried about you. So I am begging you, for everybody's sake, win her back or get over her once and for all.'

Win her back. The words reverberated around Jonas's head as he walked along the harbour wall back home—back to the house that no longer seemed so cosy, no longer a sanctuary. She had spent less than twelve hours there, yet memories of her permeated every corner, every shadow.

Lying there at night he could remember how her body fitted against his, the sound of her breathing, the silky texture of her hair as he stroked it.

How could he win her back when she'd never been his to start with? He had tried marrying her, binding her close to him with legal ties, but she had left anyway.

He stopped and looked into the inky black water broken up by the reflected light from the street lamps.

If you love someone set them free. What kind of crazy thinking was that? If you loved someone you should never let them go.

Or, just possibly, you could go with them.

He had never done that. Never supported her, taken the journey with her.

He circled slowly, looked at the village that was his only home, his whole life.

It felt like a prison.

Slowly he began walking again, his brain whirring, reliving the past once again. And it wasn't comfortable viewing. He had only visited Oxford a handful of times. The beach-bred boy had been uncomfortable with the city of dreaming spires, and he had flat out refused to go to London at all the first summer she had interned there.

Shame flooded through him. He had been her husband and he had let her down. Badly. What must it have been like for her alone, renting a room in a far-flung suburb, travelling for an hour every morning in her one good suit to work twelve hour days in a city where she knew no one? She must have been so lonely. And yet he had never visited, never surprised her by showing up unexpectedly at her door. What kind of husband did that make him?

It was cold, with a chill wind whistling in off the sea, but he barely felt it wrapped in his ski jacket—a jacket that had never seen snow because he rarely took time off work. He'd blamed her workaholic nature for their inability to stay together; he was just as bad. If he couldn't survive outside of Cornwall, away from the comfort of his home seas, then was he any kind of success at all?

And if he was destined always to live alone then probably not much of a success at all.

If he had taken a chance, moved to be with Lawrie all those years ago, would they still be together now? He'd always thought that would have spelled disaster, that she would have been embarrassed by her non-professional husband and he would have struggled to find work. Jonas shook his head. He had underestimated her. Even worse, he had underestimated himself.

He looked out into the darkness, listening to the eerie voice of the wind, the crash of his beloved surf against the harbour wall. The wind blew spray up and over and he flinched as the icy drops flicked his skin, tasted salt. His beloved home. He'd always thought his heart was right here. But, if so, why did he feel so empty?

He turned his back to the sea and with a heavy heart made his way back to the cottage, alone.

'Lawrie, we're heading up to the Hamptons this weekend. My wife would love you to come. We can introduce you around.'

The older man's expression was sincere and Lawrie felt a rush of gratitude as she shook her head.

'Honestly, Cooper, I am fine,' she assured him. 'I've worked through every weekend since I arrived, and I think it's time I got to know the city a little. Some other time, maybe, if you'll ask me again?'

'Any time,' he assured her. 'Have a lovely weekend.'

'I will,' she promised.

And she meant to—or to try at least. She had been here nearly a month; it was time to put down some roots. Buy an apartment of her own, get a cat—she'd never had a pet. Pets were a sign of belonging.

Then she'd get out more, make some friends, date. Okay, dating was a slightly terrifying prospect for an English girl who might have been married once and engaged twice but had never dated—especially New York style, whereby men seemed to think nothing of chatting to you in bookstores, in coffee shops, in lifts—*elevators*: she was a New Yorker now—and asking you out. She might have been with Hugo through most of her London life, but she was fairly sure men didn't behave like that there. It was most disconcerting.

But if dating was what it took to make her a native of New York then date she would.

But not yet.

Pulling her long cream coat on and wrapping her cashmere scarf securely round her neck, Lawrie left the office. It seemed that the whole city was heading out this weekend, and at almost seven on a Friday night the building was eerily empty. The Friday before she had worked until after ten. The Friday before that the same. The evening stretching ahead of her seemed very long and very empty.

This is the city that never sleeps, she reminded herself. *I am going to have some fun.* She could shop, she thought. Go to Barneys or Saks, buy an outfit. Go for a cocktail. A small stirring of interest reared its head in her breast. Yes, shopping. How long since she had done that?

An hour later Lawrie was feeling a little bit better. A beautiful wool wrap dress and a pair of designer leather boots had helped. *Maybe clothes will be my thing,* she thought, admiring her reflection one more time. *I'm well paid, single, and living in New York. Dressing well is a duty.*

Walking through the ground floor of the store, watching the sales assistants as they got ready to close, she found her eye caught by the displays of men's accessories. Butter-soft wallets, discreet briefcases, exquisitely cut gloves.

It wasn't just the women who knew how to look stylish in this city.

And then she saw it. A beautiful cashmere scarf. Dark greys, velvety blacks and inky purples combined in a pattern that reminded her irresistibly of a winter's night in Cornwall. Lawrie came to a sudden halt and, almost against her will, reached out to caress the soft wool. The feel of it filled her with a sudden yearning for wind, waves and the tang of salt. On autopilot she picked up the scarf and took it to the desk to be gift-wrapped, managing not to gasp when the assistant asked for a truly exorbitant amount of money.

It was Jonas's birthday in just a couple of days. It would be polite to send him a gift, surely.

Lawrie stood stock still, clutching the gift box, sudden homesickness hitting her like a punch to her stomach. She needed to snap out of it. Once New York felt like home it would all be easier. A cocktail was definitely next on the list. Possibly two.

Heading out of the store, she flung her arm out as a yellow cab cruised by. 'Taxi!'

Sometimes, no matter how good the intention, it was impossible to get in the right frame of mind. She was trying. But being perched on a high stool in the plush bar, reading the cocktail menu, watching the chattering, laughing clientele, was strangely distancing—as if she were in the audience of a play. She looked like them, these young, affluent, attractive people with designer clothes and salon-dried hair, but she was apart. Not just because she was on her own, but because she knew that all this was a charade....

Take away the dress and the heels, the artfully done make-up and the professionally glossy hair, and who was she? Lawrie Bennett, daughter of a teen mum, stepdaughter, granddaughter, young bride, divorcee. All those links and yet she was completely, utterly alone. She could disappear here and now and nobody would know until the office opened again on Monday morning.

Lawrie smiled to herself with bitter humour, imagining their shock if she wasn't at her desk by

seven-thirty, skinny latte in hand, freshly showered after a half-hour session in the gym.

It didn't have to be like this. She could do anything, grab a flight, go anywhere. Be impulsive.
Of course the last time she was impulsive she had
ended up kissing Jonas Jones, and look where
that had got her.

Well, it had got her some pretty amazing sex.
It had got her fun and laughter and time spent
with a man who understood and accepted her.

Maybe being impulsive wasn't such a bad thing
after all.

Looking up, she caught the bartender's eye and
beckoned her over. No, she wouldn't have one of
the more obvious cocktails.

'A gin gimlet, please,' she ordered. She wasn't
entirely sure what a gin gimlet was, but it made
her think of intrepid bohemian flappers, drinking gin on safari, quite possibly in the middle of
a thrilling adventure.

When was she going to have *her* thrilling adventure?

She took a sip and grimaced, but the second sip
was strangely refreshing and led quite naturally
to a third. She leant back and looked round. Op-

posite her was another lone drinker—a woman. Perfect hair, discreetly expensive clothes, sipping a cocktail while she typed busily on her laptop. It was hard to tell but she looked ten years older than Lawrie—although this *was* New York. She probably had an excellent surgeon.

As Lawrie watched her the woman looked up from her laptop and stared out at the laughing throng. An expression of such desolation, such loneliness, such sadness swept over her face that Lawrie quickly averted her eyes, embarrassed to be looking at such unvarnished pain. When she looked back the woman looked calm again, blank, coolly professional.

That could be me, Lawrie thought. *That could be me in ten years if the dates and the cat and the making an effort don't work. If I keep doing nothing but working I could make partner, be respected, be admired—and find myself drinking alone every Friday night, watching the happiness but being apart from it. Just like I am today.*

Panic caught her chest and for one horribly long second she couldn't breathe. The rush in her ears was drowning out the chatter and the laughter; her heart was swelling and aching. Was this what she wanted? Was this what she was working towards? Dinner for one and a taxi home?

Was this *living*?

She pulled out a crumpled note and put it on the table with shaking fingers, downed the rest of the cocktail—a drink that no longer seemed reckless and fun but tart and bitter—grabbed her bags and hurried out of the bar.

She managed to flag a taxi straight away and, after giving the driver her address, sat back, staring out of the window as the city changed. Shoppers and workers were making way for the partygoers, the theatregoers, the young and the beautiful, the wealthy and the stylish. The atmosphere had subtly changed to one of excitement, anticipation. It was Friday night and the city was truly waking up.

When was *she* going to wake up?

Almost panicking, Lawrie pulled her phone from her pocket and brought up her emails. Selecting an address, she began to type, jabbing at the keys in her anxiety to get it written and sent. She had to make a decision. She had to make a change. She had just seen her future, sitting across from her, and it hadn't been a pretty sight.

The clothes, the cocktails, the success. None of it mattered if she was this empty inside.

And she *was* empty. Without Jonas she had nothing.

It had only taken her nine years to work that out.

He was just relieved it was over. Spending the first Sunday lunch with his parents for twelve years had been challenging. The fact it was his birthday hadn't made it any easier.

But it had been the right thing to do. They had even smiled a couple of times.

It was odd, but it was the first time they'd ever had a celebratory dinner with just the three of them. Before, every holiday, Easter, Christmas, birthday had been spent in the hotel dining room, publicly celebrating with the hotel guests. Their whole family life played out in a public arena.

No wonder Jonas liked to be alone. He couldn't wait to get home, to relax.

But there was a party waiting for him at the Boat House, whether he wanted it or not.

It was a beautiful autumn night, although a definite chill in the air heralded the change of seasons. A perfect night for a stroll. If he parked the car back at his house he could walk along the harbour, clear his head, think about his plans one more time.

The streets leading from the harbour were narrow, twisting, but navigating them was second nature to him. On autopilot he reversed his car into a parking space and thankfully unfolded himself from the driver's seat, taking a deep breath of the cold sea air.

He stood still for a moment, gazing down the hill at the sea, lit only by the moon and stars. It was his favourite view. It made him feel alive, grounded.

He would miss it.

For one moment he stood indecisively. Home was so close. A glass of his favourite single malt, music, a good book… But he had promised Fliss.

He took a few steps down the hill, coming to a standstill as a car swung round the bend. Automatically Jonas pressed himself against the rough stone wall. Not every driver was as careful as he. The headlights were blindingly bright, sweeping up the hill as the car drew to a stop outside his house.

Who on earth could be visiting him at this hour?

A figure got out and shut the door, standing still as the car revved up and watching it drive away. A slim, graceful figure, a bag over one shoulder, another in her hand, shoulder-length hair silhouetted against the street lamp on the corner.

His heart sped up as the figure crossed to his door. And stood there.

'Lawrie?'

Rich as Cornish cream, deep as the Cornish sea.

She jumped. 'Happy Birthday.'

'You came all this way to wish me a Happy Birthday?'

'No, actually I came to bring you a present. I left it too late to post it, so here…'

She held out the box she had kept on her knee for the six-hour flight. 'Open it.'

'Out here?'

She shrugged, her eyes drinking him in as he stood lit up by the street light.

Jonas Jones. His face grey with tiredness, his hair ruffled, but so handsome, so alive, so close that her heart nearly flooded. And he was grinning as he opened the box, the corners of his eyes creased—grinning that same wicked grin she had been banishing from her thoughts, from her dreams, over and over again.

'It's a scarf,' Lawrie said shyly.

'I can see that. You really bought it for me?'

'It reminded me of you. Do you like it?'

His heart was in his eyes, so blue, so warm, so full she couldn't meet them, looking down at the dark, uneven flagstones instead.

'I love it. Is this what we do now?'

'What do you mean?'

'Buy each other scarves?'

She looked up, startled, laughed. 'Looks like it.'

'I like traditions. I think we should have one.'

'We should?'

He nodded, his eyes fixed on hers. 'A long-standing tradition. The kind grandkids find amusing and cute.'

'Grandkids?'

'I'm in favour, are you?'

Her palms were clammy, her stomach tense. Surely he didn't mean what it sounded as if he meant?

'I've never really thought about it,' she lied. Because the alternative life she could have had with him was something she liked to torture herself with on long, sleepless nights.

'Of course to have grandkids you need to have kids,' he continued, still in that calm, conversational voice whilst his eyes burned with passion. 'Shall we have kids, Lawrie?'

'We?'

Damn it, why was she croaking?

He stepped forward, took her trembling hands in his, looked down at her, and his face was filled with so much tenderness, so much hope, so much love, that she was bathed in it, suddenly calmer, suddenly braver, suddenly ready to hear whatever it was he had to say.

'I love you, Lawrie. I have loved you since you were sixteen and I have never stopped—not for a day, for a second. I was a fool to let you go once, but to let it happen twice…? If you will just let me I promise to spend every second of our future making it up to you.'

The lump in her throat had doubled in size and her chest tightened even more. She could hardly see his face through the tears in her eyes.

'I…'

His grip tightened. 'I'm too hands-on. I know that. I don't need to interview every damn gardener, every cook, source every piece of fabric, every spoon. I pay people to do that. Obviously I would need to travel back and forth, but I could be based anywhere, really. I could be based in New York. Or Sydney, Kuala Lumpur. I can be based wherever you are—if you want me to be, that is.'

The tears were spilling, falling down her face as her hands returned his grip. 'You'd move for me?'

'Anywhere. I should have it done nine years ago, but if it's not too late I will now. Please tell me I'm not too late.'

The crack in his voice nearly undid her. She was crying openly now, but laughter mingled with the tears, breaking out into a smile as she stepped into him, pressed herself against his glorious, solid strength.

'Okay.'

He put his hands on her shoulders, pushing her back to look into her eyes. 'Okay?'

'Okay, kids, grandkids, traditional scarves. I'm in,' she said. 'I'm in for the whole crazy ride. I love you, Jonas. I missed you too. There I was in this amazing place, doing my dream job, and I was so *empty* I couldn't bear it. When you didn't email, didn't call, I thought I'd missed my chance with you again. And I didn't know where to go. I thought I'd go crazy. I missed you so much. I had to come home.'

His smile, his kiss, his arms were tender as he pulled her in. 'You came home.' He grinned at her, boyish and unafraid. 'Seems only fair—after all, I see a lot of flying in my future.'

Lawrie raised her head, pressing close, lips trailing sweet, teasing kisses across his jaw, towards the corner of his mouth. 'It might not be necessary,' she whispered in between kisses.

His hand tightened possessively around her waist, drawing her closer, loosening her belt, undoing her coat buttons with his capable hands.

'Hmmm?' he breathed as he slid his hands inside her coat and under her cardigan, one hand sliding underneath her top to draw circles on her bare tummy.

She shivered.

She arched back to allow his mouth access to

her throat, to the pulse beating so insistently, desperate for his attention. 'I spoke to my firm.'

The hands stopped, the mouth moved away, and she gave a little moan of loss. 'And...?'

Damn, he wanted to talk. Talking was very overrated. 'We talked about setting up a European office. I'd still need to travel: London a couple of times a month at least, Paris, Berlin pretty regularly. But I could be based anywhere. I could be based here.'

His face lit up, love and happiness shining out. 'You'd be based here? You're coming home?'

Home. The word sounded so good.

She looked away, suddenly shy. 'If you want me to.'

'If I want? Lawrie, without you nothing works, nothing fits. If I *want*? I don't want anything else. Are you sure?'

'All this time I thought my job defined me, was all I needed. All this time I was wrong.' She stood on her tiptoes, nestled in close, seeking his warmth, his strength. 'All I need is you. You were right. I needed to be strong enough to admit it.'

Jonas shook his head, his expression rueful. 'That day at the airport I was harsh. I'm sorry.'

'You were a little harsh,' she conceded, allowing her mouth to find the strong lines of his jaw, to travel slowly towards his throat. 'But you were right too. It was unfair of me to ask.'

He looked over to the harbour at the lights shining brightly in the Boat House. 'There's a party going on at the café,' Jonas said, dropping a kiss onto the top of her head as his arms circled her. 'Or—and I would just like to point out that this is my preferred option—we could go into the cottage, barricade the doors and not come out for a week.'

'I like the idea of barricading ourselves away,' Lawrie said, smiling up at him suggestively. 'But I was hoping we could celebrate your birthday the old way: you, me, a sleeping bag and Barb, parked up on a headland somewhere? What do you say?'

His eyes were blazing with laughter, love and a promise so intense she could barely breathe.

'You said her name! I guess that means you really are back.'

'And this time it's for good,' she promised him. 'I've come home to you.'

* * * * *